Dead Man's Hand

Sixty thousand dollars in gold coin had been stolen from the Central Pacific, the second biggest train robbery in the U.S. Less than half had been recovered and the authorities wanted to know why.

When Texas Ranger Clint Anderson rode south of the border in search of the lost loot little did he suspect the trouble ahead. Pitted against corrupt rurales, bloodthirsty bandidos and back stabbers from his own brigade, whom could he trust?

And as his battle reaches a bloody and explosive climax, will he lose all?

Dead Man's Hand

John Dyson

A Black Horse Western

ROBERT HALE · LONDON

© John Dyson 2006
First published in Great Britain 2006

ISBN-10: 0-7090-8135-9
ISBN-13: 978-0-7090-8135-7

Robert Hale Limited
Clerkenwell House
Clerkenwell Green
London EC1R 0HT

Typeset by
Derek Doyle & Associates, Shaw Heath
Printed and bound in Great Britain by
Antony Rowe Limited, Wiltshire

ONE

Captain Clinton Anderson, of the newly-reformed Texas Rangers, sat his mount on a cliff of dusty shale and peered along the steep-sided ravine known as Cove Hollow. It was a desolate spot, so barren no settler cared to claim it, the haunt of coyotes and rattlesnakes. But also the hideout of desperadoes. One in particular.

'He's up there,' the young ranger muttered to himself, as he saw the high noon sun glint on steel of either a carbine or rifle barrel. 'Sam Bass and his boys.'

The cliffs rose by degrees up to a pinnacle rock and Anderson suddenly saw a puff of black powder smoke and simultaneously heard the whine of a blue whistler that sped past his head spurting dust from the cliff. Yes, it was a rifle all right, but as yet the shoot-ist up on the peak was too far off to be much of a threat.

The ranger was a lean and lanky young man of

twenty-three years, attired in a blue denim crossover shirt, a loose red bandanna around his throat, his legs encased in cowhide chaps, his feet in high-heeled boots and spurs. He was alone – or thought he was – and his plan was to try to get up close to the gunmen by pretending he might have something to offer: before he started shooting.

So he let his revolver stay in its holster, his Winchester carbine in the saddle boot, as another bullet rifled uncomfortably close making his horse, Rocky, whinny and toss his head with fright. The ranger held him steady with his knees and squinted into the sun, raking the mile of cave-riddled cliff for sign of any ambush. He took his low-crowned felt Stetson from his head, tossing his thick, fawn hair out of his eyes, and held it high to wave to whoever was up on the peak.

He saw a black-clothed figure stand up and beckon with a rifle as if inviting him to approach. That was easier said than done because it would mean finding a way through the seemingly impenetrable thorn scrub that filled the ravine and climbing up the perilous cliff side to the peak by whatever route he could find. 'It's worth a try,' he said, swinging down from the saddle and loose-hitching the horse. 'You stay here, boy.'

He was just about to slide his Winchester from the boot when he heard a sound from behind him and, turning, saw a bunch of riders weaving their way through the bare hills of these badlands and coming towards him fast.

'Aw, shee-it,' he hissed. 'I thought I'd left them behind.'

There were a dozen men in range clothes, heavily armed, led by a burly, ruddy-faced braggart with a rangers' badge pinned to his shirt – Major James B. Johnson.

'What the hell you want?' Clint, as he was known, called. 'You've sure blown my cover with all your dust.'

'What you think we want?' Johnson bellowed. 'A share of the bounty same as you. There's a thousand dollars on the head of that bozo up there. Thought you could sneak off outa Fort Worth while we was asleep an' try to collect it for yourself, huh?'

'Maybe I thought I could do better on my own than have a bumbling ass like you along,' Anderson retorted, angrily.

Johnson's alcohol-flushed face reddened even more, his eyes bulging maniacally beneath shaggy white brows, as he reined in his horse and glowered at him. 'You insolent young cow-prodder, who you think you are?' He pointed a gauntleted forefinger, threateningly. 'You use words like that to me again, you're gonna have to answer to them.'

'Anytime,' Anderson drawled, with a sigh of exasperation, levering the Winchester to snap a slug into the breech. 'You're all piss and vinegar, Johnson. I ain't seen you do much about bringing in Sam Bass so far.'

'You didn't ought talk to J.B. that way,' one of his

sidekicks, Chris Connor, sang out. 'We joined the rangers to punish Comanch' and protect the settlements, not to go pesterin' good ol' Texan boys.'

'Good ol' Texan boys.' Clint Anderson cleared his throat and spat derisively into the dust. 'They're train robbers, cowardly thieves and killers. And, besides, I need the cash.' He forced a snarling grin at them. 'Well, boys, now you're here, are you gonna help me bring 'em in, or not?'

Instead of sitting their mounts staring at him, the group of a dozen rangers jumped into action. 'How we gonna git at 'em, Clint?' Ranger Vern Wilson yelled, jumping down and checking his guns.

'The only way we can get at 'em is by going along through the scrub and making a frontal assault. We've tried before, don't think we haven't,' James B. Johnson growled. 'It's impossible to dislodge 'em. I'm willing to waste more lead if that's what Anderson wants. But remember, boys, you take orders from me, not him. I got seniority here.'

The rangers grinned at each other. It was a well-known fact there was no love lost between the two officers. They had a history.

'Come on,' Clinton Anderson growled, tugging his hat down over his eyes and pulling up his bandanna to try to shield his face from the thorns. He led the way into the ravine bottom, so narrow it was still in dark shadow. 'Let's think positive, shall we?'

The thin-faced Sam Bass, in his dusty suit, stood on

the pinnacle of rock, his rifle in his hands and looked down into the ravine. 'We got plenty of time. It'll take 'em half an hour to get along the bottom. They don't know Cove Hollow like we do. Go back down and git the hosses ready, Henry. We'll stay up here and blast 'em to hell.'

'Yassuh!' Frank Jackson hooted. 'We sure will. I allus wanted to kill me a lawman.'

'Give 'em a taste of lead, men,' young Henry Underwood urged, as he scrambled to pack up their coffee pot, tin mugs and plates, plus other oddments into a blanket, and hurried off. 'I'll be waitin' for ya.'

He had played hookey in Cove Hollow as a kid, being raised in the not too far distant town of Denton, and he knew the caves, the box canyons and back trails. Who better to lead them out?

Burly Seaborne Barnes shouldered his rifle as he took up position behind their barricade of rocks. 'Why was the first fella waving at us friendly-like?' he pondered.

'Beats me,' Sam replied. 'Guess he was tryin' to fool us 'fore the others arrived. Damned cheek of it. It's not as if I ain't spread enough cash around among the rangers. You cain't trust nobody. I thought they'd agreed to look the other way.'

'Aw, it's that new governor. Dick Coke. He's look-ing for votes,' Frank shouted. 'He's breathing down their necks. It was him put up the reward on you. Well, let's face it, Sam, you did pull off the biggest train robbery there's ever been.'

'Second biggest,' Sam corrected. 'I ain't one to lie about such thangs. It was the Reno's invented train robbin'. They took ninety thousand in '66.'

'Still, sixty thou' ain't bad, Sam,' Frank hooted. Indeed, he was barely able to comprehend the size of such a vast fortune. 'When we gonna do another? I sure got a train-robbin' itch.'

'I'm working on it, boys,' Sam said, watching the first of the rangers fighting their way out of the scrub. 'Here they come.'

In fact, nobody had been more surprised than Sam Bass when he, Joel Collins, Jack Davis and their gang, had held up the Central Pacific express when it took on water at Big Springs – out on the prairie near Ogallala, Nebraska, ten months before. They had forced their way into the Wells Fargo armoured car and been told by the conductor, who opened the safe, that the cupboard was bare.

They had been just about to leave when Joel had spotted some tin boxes in a corner. They had smashed them open and – lo and behold! – there was $60,000 all in newly-minted gold cartwheels, the kind of cash a cowboy could go out and spend, Godammit! Spend on fancy duds, fine horses, whiskey, champagne, cigars and wild, wild women which was exactly what they had done!

'Yeah,' he yelled, drawing a bead on one of the rangers, who leaped for cover. 'I got my name writ large in history. They ain't gonna catch me in a hurry.'

The best thing about it was that he still had

$13,000 stashed away. But Sam was loath to leave without staging another big robbery for folks to remember him by.

'Yeah, come on an' get us, you bucket heads,' Seaborne Barnes hollered, as the three outlaws let loose a withering fusillade of lead down at the rangers, who were hopping about like scalded cats from rock to rock. 'See if you can!'

Bullets whistled and whined about their heads as the rangers took cover and returned the lead compliments, but the boys ducked down and grinned across at each other as they reloaded their weapons. 'Quit firing,' Sam instructed. 'Let 'em get up a bit closer then we'll hit 'em with all we got.'

For half an hour Cove Hollow reverberated to the clatter of rifle fire, the whine and whistle of bullet ricochets, the echoes of explosions booming away through the steep ravine walls. But the three gunmen at the crest of the peak, from behind their pallisade of rocks, poured lead down at the rangers, unfazed by the attack.

When Vern Wilson tried to climb higher, he gave a shrill yelp and came sliding back down through the scree, clutching at his boot. 'They got me in the foot,' he gasped.

'Hold your fire,' Johnson shouted, as they dragged Vern into cover. 'Hot damn, we're gonna need a howitzer to blast 'em out of there. That position's virtually impregnable. I told the governor this would be a waste of men and ammunition.'

'Maybe I could get up above them,' Clint suggested, 'and get a shot in.'

'Oh, yeah,' Major Johnson sneered, sarcastically. 'And just how do you propose to do that?'

Anderson indicated a chimney of rock, its apex adjacent to the pinnacle of the peak. 'I might be able to get up there. Anybody got a lariat?'

'Yes.' Chris Connor offered a coil of rope. 'I brought mine.'

'I'll work my way round to its base. Give me cover when I start to climb.'

'Best of luck,' Connor called.

'He'll need it,' Johnson growled. 'We've already got one man injured. Now this damn fool wants to break his neck. Don't expect me to rescue you, Anderson. It's your hare-brained idea.'

The lanky young captain ignored him and dodged away, leaping from rock to rock and climbing up the cliffside scree as a volley from above scorched a shower of shards over him. He reached the safety of the far side of the chimney, glanced up, easing the lariat in his hands. It would require one hell of a throw. He began swinging the noose-end of the lariat and hurled it high. Maybe it was a lucky first try, but it landed neatly over the chimney point. He jerked it tight, testing it. 'Yep, here I go,' he gritted out, slinging his carbine over his back by its strap, and began to climb. It was by no means easy and he slipped and swung out into space at one point, his boots kicking air as Sam Bass and his boys spotted him and began lambasting lead his way.

'What's the matter with Johnson?' he muttered. 'Why ain't he drawing their fire?' But the thought occurred to him that J.B. might prefer to see him killed.

Clint Anderson hauled himself on up, sweat trickling into his eyes as the sun beat down on his back. Near the top of the chimney he paused, held on tight with one hand while he looped the spare rope around his waist and tied a bowline knot to hold him. He braced back on his bootheels, unslung his carbine and peered around the rock. Yes, there they were. The rangers had started another fusillade and two of the bandits were knelt firing down at them. A lean man in a black suit was moving along to a better position. It was Bass sure enough.

Clint lined up the pinhead sight in the v-notch of the carbine and squeezed out a slug. 'Hot damn!' he hissed, as, simultaneously, Bass ducked and the bullet merely sent his hat spinning. Angrily, he fired three more, but the gunmen had swung around, alarmed, turning their attention to him. The Texan tried to swing back into the cover of the chimney, but suddenly a lucky pot-shot from Seaborne Barnes cut through the rope above him and the next Anderson knew he was flying back through space. He hit the bottom hard and went cartwheeling on down through the shale scree. His head thudded against a rock and he was brought to a halt.

Sam Bass peered down but could see no sign of

the ranger. 'Come on, our ammo's getting low,' he hissed. 'Time to git outa here.'

When Major Johnson realized that the birds had flown he led his men up to the cave on the peak to take a look. All that remained was a pile of empty bullet casings. And all they could see was a plume of dust in the distance as Bass and his gang made their escape.

'Shall we go after 'em, J.B.?' one of the rangers asked.

'No. What'n hell's the use? Get Vern back to the horses ready to go. Me an' Chris will go see what's happened to Anderson,' Johnson bellowed.

Clint groaned and tried to pull himself up as the two men arrived. But his mind was spinning and he was only half-conscious as they stood over him. 'Give us a hand to get up, will ya?' he muttered.

'Sure.' Johnson gave him a vicious kick to the jaw and watched him tumble back against the rock. 'Did he say a hand or a foot?'

'You ain't gonna leave him, are you?' Connor asked.

'Sure, why not? I warned him he was on his own.'

All Clint heard was Johnson's deep-chested laughter as a black mist seemed to come over him and he slumped back.

Vern Wilson was in considerable pain but had managed to get on his mustang. 'Where's Cap' Anderson?' he asked, as Johnson and Connor emerged from the ravine.

'Aw, you know him, fat-headed as a mule,' Johnson said. 'He's gone on after 'em. Come on, let's get back to Denton. Looks like you're gonna be outa action for a bit, Vern. We need to get you to the doc.'

A young captain of rangers, Lee Hall, asked, sharply, 'What about Rocky?'

'Leave him. He's taken one of their'n,' the major lied, grinning cracked teeth at Connor. 'He'll be back for him, sometime, maybe.'

TWO

Since the end of the Civil War Texas had become notorious for its shoot-outs, murders and violence. The big ranchers who had grabbed vast tracts of land and stocked it with thousands of longhorns, left during the war to multiply and run wild, employed hired guns to move on nesters and hunt down rustlers. The Texas Rangers, many of whom had spent the war punishing Comanches, were disbanded and the victorious Federals installed a state police force, many of the recruits being recently freed blacks. These men were resented as much as the hated carpetbaggers and tax collectors who battened onto the population. In fact, three of the most feared gunmen, Clay Allison, John Wesley Hardin, and Bill Longley, were racial bigots of the worst order. Between them they had killed nearly eighty men, a large number of whom were Negroes and Mexicans.

The Texas governor, Richard Coke, had been voted into office in '76, two years before, on a law and order ticket. He had brought back the Texas Rangers, disbanded the corrupt police force, and put up rewards on the heads of the most notorious criminals. He declared it a disgrace that Sam Bass should still be roaming free and flouting the law. He called a meeting to be attended by Pinkerton detectives, bank and railroad men, sheriffs and Texas Rangers at Fort Worth Cattlemen's Club in the summer of 1878.

Wes Hardin was doing a sixteen-year stretch in the penitentiary, Longley was in the lock-up awaiting trial, and Allison, who claimed he had never killed a man who didn't need killing, had died when he got drunk and fell under a wagon. That left one last big name on the loose in Texas: Sam Bass.

When Clint Anderson regained conciousness, he hauled himself up out of the shale, weak and groggy, his shirt torn and dusty, his jaw aching, and a damp patch of blood on the back of his head. He waggled his jaw, stretched his limbs. Nothing appeared to be broken. So he found his hat and carbine and headed back along the foot of the ravine. He guessed he was lucky he had fallen in the shade or his face would have been frizzled by the sun. He hauled himself up onto the patient Rocky, took a swig from his canteen, and spurred the horse away.

The sun was sinking when he rode into Denton. He left his bronc in the livery, washed the wound on his head under a tap and brushed himself down before heading for Ryan's Saloon. There was only a smattering of men at the card tables and a couple of cowboys propping up the bar.

'Gimme one of them Budweisers,' he said.

Ryan fished a bottle out of the icebox. 'These are proving very popular since they come on the market,' the Irish proprietor remarked as he slid the bottle across. 'But I can't see them lasting. Men's tastes is very fickle.'

'I've run out of small change.' Clint tipped the bottle to his lips. 'Can you split me a fifty?'

'Sure t'ing.' Ryan dug in the cash till and produced a handful of coins among which was a golden cartwheel. 'What's happened to you? Been run over by a stampede?'

'No, I fell off a cliff.' Clint bent forward and showed the bloody cut on his head. 'Collided with a rock.'

'You oughta have stitches in that,' the 'keep said. 'Nasty cut on your lip, too.'

'Yeah, courtesy of Major J.B. Johnson.'

'Oh, it was you dey was laughing about?' The burly, moustachioed saloon 'keep stood polishing glasses with his apron. 'Called you all kinds of idjit.'

'Yeah, I bet he did. Did he tell you how he booted me in the jaw and left me lying there?'

'No, he didn't say dat. Why should the major kick you?'

'Let's say we don't get on. He's my father-in-law. Or used to be.' Anderson gave a caustic grimace. 'I cain't abide the big, blustering braggart.'

'Sounds like the feelin's mutual,' Ryan said, then

paused, studying Anderson alertly. 'Say, wasn't it you, your—'

'My wife. His daughter. He blames me for it. Hates me, you might say.'

'You were away, weren't you, so I read, when Red Bull and his war party hit your ranch? Along the Brazos someplace, wasn't it?'

'Yeah,' Clint gritted out, his eyes narrowing as he remembered finding her in the smoking ruins. The sight of that sweet girl, what they had done to her, how could he ever forget it? 'I caught up with Red Bull, blasted him to hell.'

'Good for you, pal.' Ryan stroked his brilliantined hair. 'Revenge is sweet, huh?'

'No, it ain't.' The ranger turned away so Ryan wouldn't see the tears welling in his eyes. 'It's bitter.'

To change the subject he picked up the gold twenty-dollar piece. 'You get many of these in here?'

'Sure, quite often.'

Clint Anderson recalled that the Bass-Davis train robbery haul was all in these newly minted gold coins. 'How come? Your customers don't look partic'ly wealthy.'

'Arr, that would be telling.'

Clint put his finger on the cartwheel and pushed it back across the counter. 'This could be yours.'

Ryan glanced around and lowered his voice as he picked up the coin. 'Jim Murphy was in here last night with his brother getting pie-eyed. He was pretty flush. Dat's all I know.'

'Murphy? Who is he? Where's he live.'

'Aw, they're a shiftless bunch, never done a hard day's work in their lives. They've got a rundown cabin halfway between here and Cove Hollow. Not a soul of a neighbour for miles. The boys run a few scrubby cattle. The old man's got his whiskey still. That stuff'll blow your head off.'

'You don't say.' Maybe, the ranger thought, he should pay them visit. But he had to be getting back to Fort Worth. The governor was holding a meeting and he wanted him there. As he wasn't feeling so hot, Anderson had decided to leave his horse in the livery and catch the overnight stage.

Fort Worth, as its name implied, had not long before been an adobe-walled army outpost guarding the Western frontier from Indian attacks. But by now the cruel Comanche tribes had been beaten back to the further west rugged reaches of Texas, the Llanos Estacados, or Staked Plains. Occasional war parties would still make incursions into the settled lands, as Clint Anderson had discovered to his cost, but these days Fort Worth was a bustling business township well out of the danger zone.

Clint, when he stepped from the overnight stage, realized he didn't have time to even buy a clean shirt or get a shave if he was to get to the meeting on time. The Cattlemen's Club was on the edge of town, a low-slung building with a veranda along the front. Several beef barons were taking their ease there among whom he noticed the bearded, burly Shanghai Pierce, who ran 50,000 head of cattle on half a million acres of land.

As Anderson, in his battered Stetson, his torn denim shirt and grimy bandanna, ambled towards them in his flapping cowhide chaps, and started up the steps, Pierce shouted to a waiter, 'What's that sage rat doin' comin' in here? Don't he know it's members only? Tell him the servant quarters are round the back.'

The fellow's face had a distasteful twist for his task as he hurried across and said, 'You can't come in here, suh.'

'Tell that foul-mouthed pirate, Pierce, to mind his own business,' Anderson replied. 'I'm here to see the governor.'

He pushed past and raised a middle-finger of his left hand to the rancher. 'Sage rat, yourself,' he growled.

When he first started, Shanghai had been no more than a rustler and lucky that there had been all that land, all those wild cattle to grab. It rankled somewhat that Clint, himself, had got in late on the cattle boom. After the Comanche attack on his ranch, and a year spent hunting down Red Bull and his band, Anderson had tried to revive his fortunes. But things had gone from bad to worse what with the recent nationwide slump, the crash on the banks, and no credit to be had. Clint was not the only small-time rancher who had gone to the wall.

21

That was why he had rejoined the Rangers. The pay was a pittance but there was bounty to be had. All he needed was enough to set himself up with a small ranch again.

His jinglebob spurs clinked as he strode across the polished floorboards of the club. It had an expensive and expansive air, as if nothing was too good for its clientele. There were deep leather chairs, a discreet dining area, a clicking of balls in the billiards room, and some raucous laughter coming from the bar.

'I mighta known it,' Anderson muttered. 'That buffoon's here holding sway.'

The white-moustached J.B.Johnson, glass in hand, was standing before a bunch of gents regaling them with his exploits when he rode with Nathan Forrest's Confederate raiders. Anderson had heard it before. The attack on Fort Pillow; the massacre of black Federal soldiers: to Johnson it was a great joke.

'They were nearly all drunk, sceered witless to see us coming,' Johnson shouted, drawing his revolver and waving it around. 'They threw down their arms and tried to escape. There they were running into the mighty Mississippi, trying to swim away. We potted them like sitting ducks. Pow! Pow! Pow!'

There was a look of apprehension on the faces of a couple of his audience, liberal northerners who had supported the anti-slavery cause, like Hyram Wannamaker, representing the New York National Bank of Commerce, and Sam Jones, head of the Mid-West Bureau of Wells Fargo.

'Put that gun away, J.B.,' Governor Coke cried. 'Behave yourself. Life was cheap in '64. Feelings ran high in Tennessee. Bad things were done on both sides, but it's time to put the war behind us. We're here to show a united front. It's time to impose law and order in Texas. Gentlemen, you must excuse Major J.B. Johnson, of our frontier battalion. He's a tad hot-headed.'

'I don't need no excusin',' Johnson growled, knocking back the glass of whiskey in his paw. He spotted Clint Anderson and shouted, 'Well, lookee who's here! Cain't you afford a suit and tie, Anderson? You have to come here lookin' like a saddle tramp? It don't show no respect to our eminent northern friends.'

'I got delayed, gentlemen,' Clint gritted out. 'I guess this loud-mouthed hog was hoping I wouldn't make it at all.'

'What you call me?' J.B. put aside his glass. 'I'll teach you,' he shouted, swinging a right haymaker.

Clint knocked his arm aside and his long left arm, wiry as whipcord, whipped out, smacking into the major's fleshy nose.

'Why you—' J.B. roared, as blood trickled. He started for Clint but allowed himself to be restrained by several men at the bar and stood there cussing and spluttering threats.

'Anytime you want to finish it, J.B.,' Clint said. 'I'm ready.'

'Good Lord!' a weasel-faced little man squealed. 'Is this the way you rangers behave? No wonder Sam

Bass is still at large and robbing our trains.'

The speaker was Henry Neil, manager of the Houston and Texas Central Express. 'He's hit us twice this year. He only got away with two thousand dollars, but it could be worse. Isn't it time we got some action from you hellfire heroes?'

'Aw,' Johnson bellowed, wiping blood from his nose. 'We ain't gittin' no co-operation from the populace. Sam's been spreadin' his gold around. You think dirt poor Texas folks are bothered about sixty thousand dollars missing from some New York money temple? Think again, pal.'

'Yes, and from what I hear,' the railroad man snapped, 'he's been spreading it in the rangers' direction.'

'What?' Johnson roared, his fist going to his gun butt. 'Down here that's shootin' talk, mister.'

'All right!' A ruddy-faced gent, muscles bulging beneath his check suit, jumped from his armchair. George Patterson, a Pinkerton detective spoke with a strong Scottish accent. 'This is getting us nowhere.'

He strode across to a blackboard he had set up. 'Let's look at the facts.' He scrawled up figures in chalk. ' "*Sixty thousand*" in gold coin stolen from the Central Pacific express last year. The hold-up was organized by "Three Fingers Jack Davis", a convicted train robber who has done time in the penitentiary. His share was "fifteen thousand dollars". He hasn't been seen since. Believed to be in Mexico.'

The detective passed around mug-shots of Davis.

'Surly-looking bastard, isn't he? He gets his name because he has a withered finger of his right hand. The nail of the fourth finger only reaches to the knuckle of his third. Anne Boleyn, of England, suffered from the same peculiarity.'

The chalk screeched as he wrote another '*$15,000!*'

'This was Sam Bass's share, according to our information. Likewise, none of this has been recovered, although it is probably a reduced amount by now.

'A sidekick of Sam's, Joel Collins, got "*$10,000*", as did the robber Bill Heffridge – "$10,000". They tried to make their escape together but ran into troopers and a sheriff from Dodge City. Both refused to surrender and went down shooting. That cash was found in their saddle-bags.'

The Pinkerton man looked around to make sure he had their attention. 'There were two smaller fry in the gang. They got "*five thousand*" each. Jim Berry, a former blacksmith, was shotgunned by a Missouri town sheriff. "*Three thousand*" in gold pieces was *recovered* from him. It is believed he had already frittered away two thousand in a saloon which attracted the attention of the law.'

'So that just leaves Tom Nixon,' Govennor Dick Coke put in. 'His share was "*five thousand*". But he got away across the Missippi into Tennessee. So he ain't of no interest to us.'

'That's right,' Patterson agreed, tapping the blackboard. "*Twenty-three thousand*" recovered. That leaves, with the more recent robberies in Texas, "*thirty-nine thousand* dollars" still missing. We want it back, boys. What are you gonna do about it? We want some action. Some results.'

Major Johnson looked flummoxed as he dabbed at his reddened nose. 'We've done all we dang well can. All we can do is keep on the lookout.'

The room had gone quiet as Clint scratched at the three-day stubble on his jaws, then drawled, 'What sort of new rewards you putting up?'

Dick Coke sprang to his feet and handed out wanted posters. 'There's five thousand dollars each on the heads of Bass and Three Fingers Jack, dead or alive, and a ten per-cent share of all recovered cash. This has been put up jointly by Wells Fargo, the bank, railroads and the Texan legislature.'

'Yeah, that's all very well, but how do we collect?'

'A good question, Clint,' the governor replied. 'There'll be no problem. I have full authority to pay out, I give you my word. You got any ideas?'

'Yeah, I want to work alone. I ain't taking orders from that knuckle-head, jumped-up major or not.'

When J.B. started vociferously protesting, the governor snapped, 'That's enough, Major. I'm putting Captain Anderson in charge of this operation. From now on you do what he says. So just butt out of this. Any other ideas, Clint?'

'Presumably the reward goes to whoever guns them down, whether we go in as a troop or not?'

'Agreed,' the governor said. 'That's fair. And if you

capture them alive I can assure you, after a fair trial they'll hang. That's what's going to happen to Clay Allison. The state judges agree with me on this. No more soft sentences, like Wes got. We've got to make an example of these killers.'

'So,' Major Johnson huffed, much put out by events, 'just what is the clever captain's plan of action?'

'That's for me to know and you to guess.' Clint gave a faint smile as he met his eyes. 'But what I figure we need here is a Judas goat.'

'A Judas goat?' one of the railroad men echoed.

'Yes, and I've an idea where I can find one. Thank you, gentlemen. I'll be in touch.' Clint strolled over to the bar ignoring the major. 'Meantime, how about cuttin' me out some of the coffin varnish this bozo's been hoggin'. All this argy-bargy's given me a thirst.'

When Johnson started protesting again, Governor Coke stepped over to him and warned, 'Any more trouble from you and I'll be taking you outa the field and putting you on desk duties. You're gettin' too big for your boots, J.B.'

Coke turned to the others. 'Damnably hot, ain't it, gents? How about we go out onto the veranda with our drinks and take a little air.'

They had just piled out onto the veranda when a horse-drawn surrey drew up, thoroughbreds reined in by the driver.

A middle-aged man, elegantly attired, stepped

down and offered his hand to a young woman in a dress of green, tightly waisted to accentuate her embonpoint. She held a parasol over her glossy blonde curls. Her whole being seemed to shimmer in the sunlight, unreal, like a creature stepped out of a fashion plate.

'Hey, what a looker!' Captain Lee Hall gave a low whistle that summed up the general opinion. 'I'd like to get an arm around her.'

'It's George Piper,' Governor Coke exclaimed, jumping to his feet. 'He's an oilman over at Dallas. Hi, George. You're late. You missed the main meeting, but come and join us.'

The assembled gents clambered to their feet with Southern courtesy until the lady was seated, shaking hands with Piper. When he was told about the new rewards agreed on Three Fingers Jack and Bass, he said, 'Well, I'm going to add a thousand to that.'

Clint watched the blonde settle herself in a rustle of her silk crinoline as she asked for a mint julep. The scent of her expensive perfume wafted to him, and her nicely chiselled face was powdered and heightened by rouge. Somebody had spent a fortune on her clothes, not to mention the jewellery.

Oil, that black stuff that gushed out of the ground and nobody had paid much heed to before, was, it seemed, in big demand by the factories of the north. 'Black gold,' the governor was explaining. 'It could be the next biggest thing for Texas after cows, but it hasn't really hit the headlines yet.'

'That's the way I like it,' Piper remarked. 'You have to get in first.'

He was a slightly built man of Mediterranean looks, classically handsome features, deeply bronzed in contrast to the helmet of steel-grey curls. He was decked out like a Mississippi gambler, pearl-grey frock coat, cravat, stickpin, a waistcoat of watered silk, nankeen pants and highly polished boots. All in all a couple of classy dudes. He must have been twice the age of his companion.

'What's your interest in Bass?' Clint asked.

'We met him,' the young woman exclaimed. 'We were on that train. He burst into our Pullman carriage. He nearly killed George.'

'I had a headache for weeks. He clouted me with his revolver when I tried to protect my wife.' Piper reached out his hand to clasp hers. 'He stole Kathleen's necklace, bracelet and ear-bobs. It was my wedding gift to her. We were returning from honeymoon in San Francisco. It's not just the price, though I admit that was formidable; it was a matching set of thirty-four perfectly cut rubies. It's the sentimental value. We need to try to get it back.'

'We must!' Kathleen cried, squeezing his hand in her lap. 'Are all you gentlemen going after them?'

'No, just us rangers,' Clint replied. 'Of course, they might have split the rubies up. On the other hand they might not.'

'This here's Captain Clint Anderson,' the governor said. 'I've put him in charge of the case.'

Major Johnson snorted, 'Much against my better judgement.'

Kathleen glanced at Johnson, then turned her regard onto the young ranger. Her eyes gleamed like green jewels as they met his and seemed to shoot a bolt of lightning through him. 'How do you plan to get my necklace back, Mr Anderson?'

'One step at a time,' he whispered. 'We gotta get Bass first.'

Wife? The word stymied him. The look she had given him had sent him weak at the knees. Wife! Her husband a rich man, no doubt. Ah, well, Clint thought, breaking away from her regard, so much for that. The lady was forbidden fruit, well on the other side of a fence. Not for him.

He got to his feet and touched his hat to her. 'Nice to meecha. Sooner I git started the better. We've wasted too much time already.'

'Where you going?' Johnson demanded, gruffly.

'I'm heading back to Denton to make a few enquiries. If I need your help I'll let you know.'

'Pah,' J.B. growled. 'Waste of time.'

They watched the Texas ranger, tall and broad-shouldered, stride away back into town. 'Do you really think he can get my necklace back?' Mrs Piper asked.

'I don't know,' the governor replied. 'But he's a good man. You can be sure of one thing: he'll have a durn good try.'

THREE

A hound dog bayed malevolently as the ranger approached the Murphys' dilapidated ranch house and came springing towards him, teeth bared, as he rode in. It was almost dark and the shingle-roofed shack, with its big stone chimney from which smoke drifted, had a forbidding aspect. Not a place a lone traveller would care to stop the night.

Set by a gloomy elder hung creek, there were a couple of ramshackle outhouses, a few mangy horses in a corral, and a strong smell of whiskey coming from the woods where Old Man Murphy no doubt had his still bubbling. When he and his sons weren't drinking what he produced they took it into town on their wagon to bootleg. From what he had heard they were half-drunk most of the day, but that didn't make them any less dangerous.

The 'coon hound was snarling menacingly, leaping up to snap at his boot. Anderson kicked him off and wheeled Rocky around to one of the run-down

31

outhouses. He had come prepared. He took a bit of beef jerky from his pocket, waved it to the dog and tossed it through the open door. When the hound sprang inside, he slammed the door shut and leaned across to bolt it. That dispensed with one source of trouble.

He slid his Winchester carbine from the boot and rode forward to the shack. 'Anybody home?' he shouted.

The old man opened the front door and stepped out, or rather, swayed, holding onto the door jamb for support, a shotgun clutched in his other fist. 'Who the hell is it? Whadda ya want?'

'I want Jim Murphy and his brother Bob. Tell 'em to come out, their hands up. I'm a Texas ranger and I've warrants for their arrest.'

'On what charge?'

'Harbouring Sam Bass, a notorious criminal.'

Murphy's whiskey-reddened face was contorted with anger, his words slurred, as he hurled obscene oaths. 'Get outa here. You ain't taking my boys.'

'Put that scatter-gun down or I'll take you in, too,' Clint shouted. 'Be sensible.'

A window was broken and a rifle-barrel poked through. Anderson didn't wait to argue. He spurred Rocky hard, hauling him to the left, and went leaping away as the old man came up with the twelve gauge. There was a roar and a flash as pellets sped past the horse's rear.

Clint galloped away to the back of the corral,

leaped from the saddle and loose-hitched Rocky to a post. 'So that's the way they want it, is it?'

He ducked down and made a run for cover as a slug from the rifle at the window whined past his head. He watched the old man tumble backwards drunkenly as he fired his second barrel. One of the boys struggled to pull him back into the house.

Clint didn't want to kill them, just scare them. He needed them alive for questioning. He squeezed out a shot from the carbine and 40 grains of powder powered out a .44 calibre bullet to smash through the plank wall of the cabin above their heads. He levered the twelve-shot Winchester with expert rapidity and sent a line of bullets crashing into the shack. 'That should make 'em hit the deck,' he muttered.

'Throw out your guns. You're surrounded,' he yelled. 'Or do you want the rest of my boys to pepper you like a colander? We're gonna give you to the count of fifty to come on out.'

He scurried away through the dusk to the back of the shack. He had brought two rawhide lariats along, retrieved from his saddle horn and stuffed the empty carbine back in the boot. He spotted a pile of old sacks. 'Just what I need.'

All was quiet at the front of the shack. He couldn't see any sign of life at the back, so he went up close, whirled the lariat to fall over the chimney stack, pulled it tight and hauled himself up. He reached the chimney and stuffed the sacks down. 'That should smoke the polecats out.'

He made the other lariat tight around the sturdy stone chimney and made nooses on the tail ends of each rope. He paid them out and slid down the other side of the steep roof, leaning back at the edge and waiting results.

There was a lot of coughing and cursing from inside as acrid woodsmoke began to billow from the broken windows. Suddenly the younger brother, Bob, burst out of the door firing a revolver wildly at imagined enemies. Clint waited until he had loosed his six, dropped his lariat loop neatly over his shoulders, and heaved the wiry little Irishman up into the air. He hauled him up tight and buffaloed him with the butt of his Peacemaker. Bob instantly ceased his protestations and was left to dangle there.

'What the divil's going on?' Jim Murphy edged out of the door to investigate, hardly able to see through the smoke and gloom. The ranger spun the second lariat and lassooed him, too, pulling his elbows into his sides. But before he had time to take up the slack the old man stumbled out, swung the reloaded shotgun in his direction and let loose.

Pain seared into Clint's right arm as pellets from the volley caught him. He was lucky he wasn't in the full path of the blast. The only thing he could do before the old man fired again was instinctively leap forward from the roof. His boots caught the middle-aged Murphy in the chest, knocking him to the ground. He tumbled clear, transferring his Peacemaker six-shooter to his left hand and, his right arm burning like fury, came up on one knee, aiming it at Jim, who was trying to free himself from the rope. He had an old Dance Brothers revolver in his hand, which he was fumbling to use.

'I wouldn't if I were you,' Clint hissed out, wincing at the pain in his arm. 'Unless you feel lucky.'

The ranger knocked the revolver from Jim's fist and, hearing a curse, turned to see the old man trying to get to his feet. He kicked him sharp in the teeth and put him back down again. He stooped to retrieve the shotgun and tossed it into a water butt.

'Right, y'all,' he gasped out, surveying them and keeping the Peacemaker steady. 'I'm minded to hoist you varmints up by your necks here and now.'

The two brothers whined, coughed, and protested, pleading their innocence. Clint pistol-whipped Jim, knocking him to the ground. He shot through the rope above Bob, letting him fall to the floor. 'On your feet, all of you,' the ranger shouted. 'Ye're gonna hitch a hoss to your wagon. Then I'm taking you into Denton.'

Anderson glanced at the blood seeping through the torn denim shirt of his right arm. 'Damn you! Look what you've done. I swear, you make one more false move and I'll have no hesitation in sending y'all to Kingdom Come.'

His troubles, however, weren't yet over. The old man was stumbling and cursing. Every time he tried to clamber onto the wagon he fell back and sprawled in the dust. He was too drunk to do anything but moan, 'Please don't take my boys. What'll I do without dem?' His antics were such Clint, in spite of the nausea, the shock of the wound and spasms of dizziness that hit him, could barely restrain an embittered grin.

'What'n hell have I got myself into? Things aren't going right on this assignment. All right' – he pointed the revolver at the father – 'you stay here. But if you ever take a shot at me again it'll be the last thing you do.'

He climbed up onto the back of the wagon and told the two brothers on the front box to get moving and not to try any tricks. As they moved out he shouted back at the older Murphy, 'Don't forget to feed that damn dawg.'

'Here,' Jim Murphy called, taking a swig from a jug he had found under the seat as his brother set the horse off at a trot. He passed it back. 'You better dose that wound. It don't look good. We don't want you dying on us, Ranger.'

Clint took the jug and splashed it over the torn flesh of his upper right arm, gritting his teeth against the stab of pain. 'Might as well take a drop myself,' he said, settling down against the backboard of the wagon.

Two slugs of the poteen and his head really was reeling. 'Here,' he called to Jim, pulling off his bandanna. 'I'm losing a lot of blood. Can you git back here and tie this tight around my damn arm?'

He guessed, thinking about it later, that the

Irishman could have easily clubbed him and made his escape. But, now the shooting was over, he seemed resigned to his fate. In fact, he sat down beside him and took a few more sups from the jar as they rattled back on the rocky track under the icy stars.

When they reached Denton he even helped the ranger down, although Anderson, his mind wavering, kept his revolver vaguely on them both. He led them into the sheriff's office and called, 'Hey, lock these two birds up. They gave me a bit of trouble.'

Then, after he had watched Sheriff 'Hutch' Hutchison lock the brothers in separate cells, Clint whispered, 'Thanks, I'll—'

He didn't finish the sentence as his knees buckled and the floor came up to hit him.

Hutchison looked down at him. 'Well, I'll be doggoned. Guess I'd better go get the medic.'

Sam Bass rode into Elder Creek on his fast little pony, Jenny, and found Old Man Murphy by his whiskey-still taking the best cure he knew for a splitting hangover, another morning cup of the fiery brew.

'Howdy, Sam,' he greeted. 'Welcome y'are, but I got terrible news. My boys are in jail. Some ranger came and arrested 'em. We gave him a lead reception but he was too crafty for us. The bastard loosened my last couple of teeth.'

'They came after *us*,' Sam said, sitting his horse, 'but we gave 'em the slip. Things are getting too hot to handle around here. I've come for that cash I hid.'

'Sure, I wouldn't know where that is.' Murphy, in a filthy vest and pair of pants held up by a bit of rope, scratched at his scruffy beard and took another sup of moonshine. 'They ain't told me nuthin'.'

'Well, *I* do. It's in your chimney breast and I'm taking it 'fore Jim and Bob spill their guts to the rangers.'

'Sure, they wouldn't do dat,' Murphy protested. 'Haven't we always given you shelter here? We're Irish rebel boys, Sam. We have no truck with the authorities. Don't you worry. Your secrets are safe with my boys. We go back a long time.'

'I know. Don't think I ain't grateful, but look what I found stuck on a telegraph post.' He tossed Murphy a wanted poster with his photograph on it. 'I'm more famous than Jesse James. I bet they ain't got five thousand on *his* head.'

'Five t'ousand! Jeez, that's a lot of gilt.' Murphy studied the poster and growled, 'Ach, what you got to worry about? D'is don't look nuthin' like you.'

It was true. The picture was a studio portrait Sam had sat for in Deadwood City after he and Joel had sold some stolen cattle and were tasting the good life in the Black Hills of Dakota. He was togged out in a fancy four-button suit, celluloid collar and tie, his hair waved and pomaded, his moustache waxed into fashionable twirls.

Murphy cackled, 'You look like some Eastern tinhorn.'

'Too true.' Sam had long ago discarded the collar and tie, his suit was stained and concertinaed, his hair thick with dust hung over his razor-sharp features, and the moustache drooped disconsolately. 'A man can't keep up appearances when he's on the run.'

Old Man Murphy's eyes glimmered greedily as he read the small print where the reward could be claimed, or information sent, by writing to the Texas governor at Dallas, the Union Pacific Railroad Express, Omaha, or the Pinkerton Detective Agency, Chicago.

'If you're thinking of trying to turn me in,' Sam said, patting the Smith & Wesson self-cocker stuck in his belt, 'it wouldn't be advisable.'

'Turn you in? You're jokin'! Ye're more to me than my own sons. I'd never betray you, Sam. I swear that on my wife's grave, and that goes for the boys, too. Ye've been like a brother to them.'

'Come on.' Still on horseback, Sam led the way back to the ranch house. He jumped down by the chimney stack, took out his knife and began prising out one of the stones. He stuck his hand into the hole and pulled out a pair of long johns, the ankles knotted and strung tight at the waist. The bulky legs bulged and clinked as he weighed the bundle in his fist. 'Seems like you been helpin' yourselves.'

'Jim's had no more than one cartwheel a week like you said he could, I swear to that. Dat was the agreed payment.'

Sam tipped out the sparkling gold cartwheels, coinage of the San Francisco mint of 1877, the previous year, and counted them out into neat $100 piles.

'Thirteen thousand and sixty dollars,' he concluded. 'That's more than one a week gone missing, but what the hell!'

He tossed the old man a cartwheel. 'There's another for your trouble.' He packed the coins into his saddle-bags. 'We're doing one last job, then we're headin' for Mexico.'

What coins he couldn't get in the saddle-bags he tied tight in the long johns and slung over Jenny's neck. He didn't much care to have to carry the cash around; it was heavy and bulky and a man never knew who he might run into. But, needs must.

'Sure, I nearly forgot. There's a letter come for you.' Murphy went inside and found the missive, handing it across. 'Dat's postmarked Mexico, too.'

'Yeah, so I see,' Sam muttered as he read it. 'It's from Three Fingers Jack. Sounds like he's doing fine south of the border. Got himself a house and ranch, living a life of luxury.' Sam tucked the letter in his pocket and swung back onto Jenny. 'So long, old-timer. You be sure to tell your boys what I said.'

He spurred the pony out of the hollow and set off at a steady lope west. He had a 100-mile ride before him to the town of Bowie where he had agreed to meet up with his gang. As he rode he dwelt on the words of Three Fingers Jack.

What are you doing hanging around Denton for? Why don't you put your toothbrush in your back pocket and come south to join me? You know it makes sense. We were a good team. But I should warn you it might not be so easy getting across the border. Apart from bounty hunters, rangers and lawmen on the lookout for you Stateside, over here there are bands of rurales *on the prowl, worse than the packs of bandits they are supposed to be hunting. So, my advice to you is to send your capital on ahead. There's a stage service now running through Eagle Pass which links up with another this side of the Rio Grande bound for Piedras Negras. I'll pick it up at the depot and keep it safe until your arrival. Just stick it in a trunk so it don't look suspicious. In the meantime I'll be scouting around for a nice little hacienda for you and stock it with some sweet* señoritas *to attend to your every whim. . . .*

The more he thought about it, the more it made sense. In fact, Sam was quite excited by the prospect of making a new life. Wouldn't he have enough to carry on horseback from the proceeds of the new robbery he had been planning? From what he had heard it would be *big*. Could he trust Jack Davis? Sure he could.

'I got the world by the tail,' Sam cried. 'I'll be leaving Texas with a bang!'

When he reached Bowie he went into a hardware store to see what was on offer. He purchased a plough share, took it back to his hotel room to pack in straw in a strong wooden box, tucking his gold into the crannies and nailing the lid tight. He stuck labels on: *Contents: plough share and assorted machine pieces*, and addressed it to 'Señor J. Artemio, at Piedras Negras, Mexico.' He got a boy to help him heft it to the stage depot, paid for the box by weight and mileage, and tucked the receipt in his pocket.

He was watching the six-horse stage set off for Fort Worth and onto Waco, Austin, San Antonio, Uvalde, Crystal City and Eagle Pass, through to the Rio Grande, when Seaborne Barnes and Frank Jackson rode in. Sam grinned at them, raised an outstretched hand to slap at theirs and yelled, 'Wish the stage luck, boys. It's got a long way to go.'

'What you lookin' so pleased about, Sam?' Seaborne asked. 'Like you're the cat who got the cream.'

'I surely did,' Sam laughed, 'an' there's gonna be more. You can count on that.'

FOUR

The sun hit him like a furnace when he stepped out from Brown's Hotel in Denton, where he had spent an uneasy night. The bandaged wound on his right arm pounded painfully where the doc had picked shot from his torn flesh. And his head pumped in unison from the Murphys' foul whiskey. He needed to buy a clean shirt and pants and wash away the dirt and grime. So, after he had soaked in a hot tub for half an hour and the barber had scraped away a week's growth of stubble, he felt like a new man.

'All I need now is a cool beer to straighten me out,' Clint muttered, heading for Ryan's saloon.

He had tossed away his blood-encrusted bandanna, along with his old duds, and had bought a fancy purple on grey polka dot neckerchief to set off his new blue shirt and jeans.

'Right, I got work to do,' he said, as he chewed through a ham roll for a late breakfast and drained his glass, sliding it back along the bar. 'I'd better go see the boys.'

The burly Sheriff Hutchison gave him a self-satis-fied smirk as he entered the jailhouse. 'Me and my two deputies been softening 'em up for you. It's time those two hooligans got some sense knocked in their heads.' Clint hadn't requested such strong-arm tactics, but he guessed it wouldn't do any harm if he now played the good guy.

'Howdy, Jim,' he said, as he was let into the small adobe cell. 'Hope you ain't been roughed up too bad.'

Murphy was sat on his bunk, his head bowed over his knees, his long hair lank over his face. When he looked up, with a grimace of pain, there was blood trickling from his swollen lips and he could hardly see out of one eye. He mumbled a barely audible curse and clutched his ribs.

'That's a nice shiner they've given you. Hey, boy, don't look so miserable. Have a cigarette. Jeez, I thought you were made of tougher stuff. I can't see you surviving five years on the chain gang.'

'What?' Jim croaked, as Clint lit the cigarette for him. 'What you talking about?'

'Aw, the governor's cracking down on crime. He's told me that's the least you'll get. Harbouring dangerous criminals, passing stolen cash, those are the charges, not to mention attempted murder of a peace officer, namely myself, and resisting arrest. I'm afraid you're for the high jump, Jim.'

'I ain't done nuthin'. We t'ought you was an armed robber attacking us, dat's why we fought back.'

'No use denying it, Jim. Your brother Bob's already

spilt his guts. He told us all about how you've been helping the Bass gang.'

'That's a dirty lie.' Jim's fingers were shaking as he fumbled with the cigarette. 'Jesus, you ain't got a bottle with you, have you? I need a drink.'

'You won't be getting no hard stuff over the next five years. The only hard stuff you'll be getting is from those cons they toss you in with. They're gonna welcome a nice piece of trash like you. Whoo! Fancy spending every night for five years locked up with those brothers. I sure don't envy you, Jim.'

Clint paused to let it sink in, seeing by the sick look on Murphy's face that he had already landed his fish. 'Of course,' he said. 'You help us. We'll help you.'

'I don't blow on my pals. That ain't our code.'

'Ah, well, I'm sorry to hear that because Governor Dick Coke has come up with a package whereby all charges could be dropped against you and your family. You don't really want us to pull your old man in, too, for peddling moonshine, do you? He's too old to do time. It would kill him.'

Anderson got up to leave, saying, 'Can't hang around. It's a lovely morning out there. Just imagine how nice it would be to be free, Jim. You could go over to Ryan's and wet your whistle.'

As he banged on the door and called to the sheriff to let him out, Murphy looked up and moaned, 'Hang on, Ranger. Let's hear first, what do you want me to do?'

'It's simple.' Clint shrugged his shoulders and smiled at him. 'All you've got to do is ingratiate yourself with

Sam and keep us informed of what he is up to.'

'How can I do that?'

'Easy.' The ranger jotted down a name and address. 'This is where you send a cable to us as soon as you get any information. All you gotta do is join the gang and go along on their next raid. Let us know what's happening and we'll do the rest.'

'That's crazy, mister. If they suspect me they'll shoot me dead.'

'So, you'll have to act the part. Just stand back when they strike.'

'What about the reward?' There was a furtive, feral look in Murphy's eyes. 'If I provide the information that should be mine.'

'You're a greedy li'l gofer, aincha? You, your brother, your father, will be granted immunity from prosecution. What more do you want? OK, I'll throw in five hundred dollars for you, if and when we succeed.'

'Make it a t'ousand.'

'All right,' Clint sighed. 'A thousand. That's our final offer.'

'Dat's better.' Jim licked at the blood dripping from his lip. 'How do I know I can trust you?'

'Some of us were raised honest in these parts. The governor's word is his bond. So's mine.' Clint extended his hand. 'Shake on it, pardner.'

Murphy spat on his palm and gripped Clint's hand. 'What now?'

Sheriff Hutchison was opening up. 'Somebody call me?'

'Yep,' Clint drawled. 'They're both free to go. Don't breathe a word of this to anyone, sheriff. Or you, Jim. Not even to your brother. That way you get to stay alive.' He slapped the Irishman's shoulder. 'Make sure you telegraph us. Soon. Good luck.'

'Sure,' Murphy muttered, 'I'm gonna need some.'

When he went back to the hotel to settle his bill, Anderson suddenly felt as if his legs were going from under him and held onto the desk to steady himself.

'You OK?' Reg Brown, the hotel keeper asked.

'Yeah. It was just a dizzy spell, made my head spin.'

'The doc said you oughta lay up for a coupla days. You lost a deal of blood.'

'Aw, I ain't got time. I need to get back to Fort Worth.'

'Why not put your feet up for an hour or two? We ain't in need of the room.'

'Yeah, maybe I will take a li'l rest. Leave tonight when it's cooler.'

He climbed the stairs, entered the room, pulled the curtain across the open window, unslung his gunbelt and hung it from the brass knob of the bed. He pulled off his boots and stretched out. He removed his new shirt and took a look at the bandage on his arm. All he needed to do was keep the wound clean and let it heal. He poured himself a glass of water from the jug and propped himself against the pillow.

His mind drifted back to his boyhood, the farm in the woods of east Texas. He had been six when the

47

Civil War broke out and his father had gone off with his musket to fight for the South. Just one of the poor bloody infantry, one of the multi-thousands who got blown to pieces in the slaughter. When he didn't come home his mother had married again, but Clint had not enjoyed the reign of his stepfather, a hard, bitter, drinking man. When he was fourteen he lit out and started drifting, taking what work he could find. He was a natural horseman, a reasonable shot, fast with his fists and could take care of himself. He had joined a cattle drive north, sure enough a rough rite of passage into adulthood.

Crossing the treacherous quicksands of the Red River out of Texas was the easy part. Hours spent in the wet saddle in torrential downpours and lightning storms, nothing but bread and coffee, constantly wet and cold, horses giving out, ague, fever, blisters, hauling cattle out of the mud, barely any sleep, nightherding, constantly on the alert, staying awake by rubbing tobacco in the eyes: men had to be hard to endure. When Comanches stampeded the longhorns it was the first time he had had to aim his revolver with intent to kill. There had been many times since. By the age of sixteen and roistering with the loose ladies of Dodge City, he guessed he could count himself a man.

Clint had drifted far north into the Rockies, lived with the Utes for a while, mingled with trappers, gold hunters, gunslingers in Denver and Santa Fe. But, wearied by the wandering life, he had returned to

Texas. He wanted to make something of himself. By the age of twenty he had started a small herd on a nice spread of land along the Brazos on the edge of the frontier. He had axed trees, built his own cabin, and things looked rosy, especially when he met Mary and fell for her hook, line and sinker. She was the only daughter of the famous, or infamous, former ranger, Major James B. Johnson, who had become a legend in Texas fighting the Comanche before he went off to the war. But Johnson didn't see eye to eye with the young upstart, Anderson, and he certainly didn't intend to give him his daughter.

'What the hell have you got to give her?' he sneered. 'You're just a dead-beat. I want a richer man for my girl.'

Mary, however, had had her fill of her father's loud-mouthed bluster and ran off with Clint. By the time he caught up with them it was too late. They were wed in a small baptist church and were living blissfully together on their small ranch. Yes, they had had two good years, close as two peas in a pod. Then she became pregnant with their child. Bliss, indeed, until that night – he had been away for three days buying horses – and came back to the smoking ruins, the blood. . . .

Those were images that constantly returned to shatter his mind, haunt him. Maybe it was time he found himself a new woman. Once he had raised some cash to start again he would. Clint, as he lay there, couldn't help his thoughts drifting to the lovely Kathleen. Why? What point was there in thinking of her? She was another man's woman, legally tied to him. The wife of a wealthy man. It was against his principles to get involved with such a one. Anyway, she couldn't hold a candle to Mary. It wasn't love. It was lust, that sheer stab of electricity that had hit him, that made him think of her. . . .

How, he wondered, had Piper come to meet her? Maybe going up the Mississippi on board a paddle steamer from New Orleans. There were plenty of good-looking 'hookers' who targeted rich men on those trips. No, he was probably misjudging her. Maybe she was a nice girl from a good family who would obviously want the best match for her. Maybe. . . .

He had closed his eyes and started to drift into sleep when he heard a light tapping on the door. 'It's open,' he called, but could hardly believe his eyes when he saw Kathleen. No, he thought, I must be hallucinating. He closed them again and heard her say, 'I've been worried about you.'

'Jeez!' he exclaimed. 'Where did you spring from. I was just thinking about you.'

Kathleen drew back a veil that hung from a gaudy hat, and gave him a slight smile of her rouged lips. 'We were visiting the rangers' office in Fort Worth and the news had come through on the telegraph that you had been shot. So, here I am.'

Her petticoats beneath an expensive yellow silk costume rustled as she sat gingerly on the side of the bed. 'Don't look so alarmed. I came on the spur of the moment. My husband had to go to Houston on business for a few days. So, I caught the stage to Denton. Are you OK?'

'Sure, Old Man Murphy winged me with his scatter-gun, thassall. Everything's going fine.' He reached out and gripped her arms above the elbows as her powder and perfume tingled his nostrils and he felt a stirring in his loins. 'I really thought I was dreaming. You're real!'

'Yes, very much so.' She reached out a gloved hand and touched fingers to his suntanned chest, running them up to his shoulder. 'It doesn't look too serious. Now I know that you're OK I'll be getting back. There's a stage out at six. We don't want any scandal, do we?'

'No, we sure don't. This ain't a good idea, Kathleen.'

'I don't usually do this sort of thing. It was just that horrible Major Johnson was roaring with laughter about you, saying it served you right; you thought you could do everything on your own, stuck your nose where it wasn't wanted, and deserved to be buckshot. He made me mad.'

'Yeah, J.B. and me ain't the best of pals.'

'I had better go,' she murmured, starting to rise.

Clint held her still. 'What's the hurry? You've got plenty of time. Or should I say we have?'

'I am trying to travel incognito,' she whispered, huskily, taking off the veiled hat and casting it aside. 'I don't want—'

'Nor do I,' he muttered, 'but sometimes there

ain't nuthin' you can do about it.'

'No,' she protested, as he drew her to him, but her lips were soft, sultry and responsive as he kissed her. 'Oh, my God,' she moaned, 'I couldn't stop thinking about you.'

'Do me one favour. Go over and turn the key in the lock. Then take your costume off.'

'*No*, Clint.' She shook her head, vehemently, saying, 'I mustn't. It's not fair to George. It's not right. We—'

'We've got four hours. Why else have you come here?'

'Oh.' She gave a deep sigh and did as he bid. She took off her costume top and unbuttoned her skirt at the back and let it rustle to her feet. She stood there in her lacy underclothes, kicked off high-heeled slippers to give a glimpse of gartered black stockings, and a flash of white thigh. She stepped towards him, smiled widely, showing white teeth, the tip of a pink tongue, her green eyes sparkling with wickedness, and settled down on top of him, as gently as a dove settling on her nest. 'Have you found my necklace yet?' she asked.

'No,' he murmured, as he kissed the soft whiteness of her breasts. 'But I'm on the case. You can assure your husband of that.'

FIVE

Sam Bass was proud of the fact that since he had turned outlaw he had never had to kill a man in cold blood. Of course there had been that unfortunate incident when they first turned to highway robbery up at Deadwood. The first four coaches they stopped all proved to be fresh out of booty, or the passengers were so poor the boys ended up digging in their own pockets to buy them breakfast. But then the stage from Cheyenne came along and the damn fool driver didn't stop at their command. One of the gutter trash Bass had along panicked and blasted him from the box. After banishing the culprit from his gang Sam had decided robbing *trains* might be more profitable.

Maybe it was because he was no dyed-in-the-wool killer, posed no real threat to the local populace, that Sam was so popular. When he, Seaborne Barnes and Jackson, clattered into the Bowie saloon, there were looks, not so much of apprehension, more admiration on the faces of the men idling there. There were smiles all round when Bass slapped down a gold twenty piece and announced that drinks were on him.

'Where's Henry gotten to?' he asked, as he leaned on the bar and wet his own whistle.

'Aw, he's got the hots for some *señorita* up at Wichita Falls,' Jackson replied. 'He said he's had enough of kicking his heels at Cove Hollow.'

'That's his bad luck because the next strike's gonna be big.' Sam lowered his voice and led them over to a corner table where they wouldn't be overheard. 'I've got it on good authority that there's at least twenty thousand dollars in the bank at Round Rock.'

'How do you know that?' Frank Jackson asked.

'From the horse's mouth. One of the bank tellers got the boot for being impertinent. He was in the saloon getting drunk. He told me Shanghai Pierce, himself, banks there and had just paid in the proceeds from his cattle drive. Shanghai don't trust paper money and insists on gold. This is gonna be a pushover, boys. We just walk in and help ourselves.'

The bearded Seaborne beamed at him. 'You sure about this, Sam?'

'Sure I'm sure. The sooner we get there, the sooner we're rich. The trouble is we could do with another couple of boys in case of trouble. At least someone to hold the hosses if Henry ain't along.'

'Aw, why worry? We can do it.'

Jackson grinned, greedily. 'All the more for us if we split three ways. That's the way I want it, Sam.'

'Sure, equal shares, even though I'm the one who has to do all the thinking.' Sam shrugged and poured whiskey from the bottle all round. 'It sure is funny, ain't it?'

'What is?' Seaborne asked.

'Money. The more a man has the more he seems to want. Look at me. All I inherited when my daddy died was a saddle and a bull calf. I got a fortune that'll be waiting for me in Mexico, but I still want more.'

Seaborne was the tubby, jovial one of the bunch. 'You're just greedy,' he laughed. 'Thassall.'

Frank Jackson was a more lean, mean, taciturn man. His Stetson, which he rarely removed, cast shadow over his face as he muttered, 'No, it's gold fever. No man's immune.'

'That's why I've gotta make this my last job in Texas. Now they've put these rewards up on me I cain't trust nobody.' The outlaw glanced around the saloon. 'Not even these good ol' boys.'

Sam had hesitated about leaving Texas up to now. All his family were in the Denton area and he felt somehow responsible for them. His mother had died giving birth to her tenth child. Sam and his siblings, both parents gone, had been taken in by their Uncle Dave, a stern taskmaster. But Sam, for one, hadn't taken to having Christianity larupped into him.

No, he had never been one of Denton's better

boys. He had taken to racing his fleet little pony, Jenny, for prize money and drifted from town to town. Then he had hooked up with Joel Collins, who had persuaded him to steal a herd of cows. It was the start of his lawless life. They had headed north to Dakota where they had met Three Fingers Jack. Up to then Sam and Joel had been bungling amateurs. Jack was a real criminal, with form. It was Jack who had arranged the Central Pacific robbery, who showed them the ropes. Now Joel was dead. It was time to shake the dust of Texas off his boots, go south of the border to join Jack.

Clint Anderson watched from his bedroom window as Kathleen Piper, in her yellow silk costume, strolled, her wide hips swinging, across the dusty street to the stage that had drawn up outside the Denton Wells Fargo office. Her face was shaded by her parasol and the spotted veil that hung from her little brown hat. But men and women gave her curious glances as she climbed inside. They could hardly not notice such an exotic creature.

'This is crazy,' he said to himself. He felt drained by the afternoon's activity, coming down from the heights, coming to his senses. She had been good. An oasis in the desert. A very sexy lady. An expert at the game. But it was a *dangerous* game. 'She's quite a gal,' he whispered. 'Why do I have the feelin' she's gonna be trouble?'

When the stage, with half a dozen folks on top,

had headed off for Fort Worth and all stops south, the ranger buckled on his gunbelt and went downstairs.

Brown was at the desk and glanced at him, an amused twinkle in his eye. 'Feeling better now?'

'Yep.' He nodded. 'You could say.'

Clint strolled along to the telegraph office and sent a cable to Governor Coke.

JUDAS GOAT IN OUR POCKET STOP PROMISED IMMU-
NITY STOP HOPEFUL OF QUICK RESULT STOP ANDER-
SON.

He fortified himself with a steak and fried eggs in a restaurant then went to collect Rocky at the livery. It was a long sixty miles haul back to Fort Worth but if he kept up a steady lope he could be back there by the morning.

The three outlaws made their way back to Cove Hollow for Sam wanted to pick up some bits of jewellery gleaned from passengers on the Central Pacific hold-up which he had hidden in a hole under a rock.

'Nearly forgot about this little lot,' he said, as he pulled out a gunny sack. 'They've been here since last year. We should be able to raise some cash on 'em at a pawnbroker's.'

He tipped the trinkets onto the ground by their camp-fire. 'There ain't nuthin' much, just watches, rings, baubles, bangles and beads. I did relieve some classy dame in a Pullman of a ruby necklace set in gold, but I lost that to Three Fingers Jack in a card game.'

'There's somebody coming up the ravine,' Seaborne shouted out, raising a rifle to his shoulder and taking aim. 'If it's that nosy ranger back again—'

'Hold your fire,' Sam said, taking a look. 'It's Jim Murphy,'

'What's he doing here?' Jackson growled. 'I thought the rangers had arrested him.'

It was indeed Murphy. He was climbing up the steep ravine on foot, leading his mustang. When he saw them he held aloft a quart earthenware jug. 'I've brought you some whiskey, boys,' he hollered.

'I don't like it,' Jackson hissed. 'I never did trust that booze-besotted family. Maybe he's working for the rangers.'

'No, he's one of us,' Sam said, signalling with his carbine. 'Come on up, Jim.'

Murphy was out of breath by the time he reached them. 'Hey, fellas,' he gasped, 'ye're certainly well hid. I t'ought I'd never find you.'

'What brings you here, Jim?' Sam asked, taking a hit from the jug. 'Everything OK? The old man said the rangers had taken you.'

'Aw, they gave me hell,' Murphy moaned, pointing to his black eye. 'They put me through the mincer. But they didn't get nuthin' outa me. Not a peep.'

'So, why are you here?' Jackson demanded.

'Jasus, I've had enough of sittin' on my backside gettin' nowhere. I want to join you boys.' Murphy appeared highly nervous, unable to hold their regard, glancing askance as if he'd got a buzzard sitting on his shoulder. 'Those rangers give me the creeps. I want to get my own back on those bastards for the way they treated me and my brother.'

Frank Jackson gave a scoffing laugh. 'Maybe they sent you to sniff around. Maybe you're some slimy, double-crossing sewer rat, is my opinion.'

He was toting a converted Spencer carbine .50 calibre, favoured by buffalo hunters, which packed a powerful punch, and turned it threateningly on Murphy. 'I don't believe a word this scumbag says.'

'I swear on my mother's grave' – Jim anxiously crossed himself – 'every word I say is the God's honest truth. Come on, Sam, I've been like a brother to you. Don't let him speak to me like that. Didn't I look after your cash?"

'True.' Sam sounded a tad disbelieving himself. 'You mean you want to come in on a raid?'

'Dat's what I'm here for.' Murphy pulled an old sawn-off Dance Brothers storekeeper from the pocket of his tattered cowhide coat. 'Look, I got a gun. I know how to use it and I'm eager to back you boys. Ain't that enough?'

'He couldn't hit a barn door with that thing; he's never sober,' Jackson warned. 'He's no use to us, Sam.'

Sam sucked his teeth. There was no doubt they

were short on manpower.

He didn't see why Murphy couldn't make himself useful. 'Ah, you're a suspicious old woman, Frank. Jim's all right.' He grinned at the Irishman. 'We ride south tonight to Round Rock.'

They rode their horses at an easy pace, not wishing to tire them, and by noon the next day holed up in a hick town called Taylor. It was a town like any other out on the sere Texan plain. They filled their bellies, had a few drinks, then Sam said they should book into the town hotel and get a few hours' shut-eye before moving on in the evening. 'That way we'll be in Round Rock by tomorrow morning.'

The hotel was a run-down joint with a notice on the wall instructing, 'Spurs must be removed in bed.' They took off their boots and bunked down two to a bed, the shades drawn against the blaze of sunlight outside.

After a while, Murphy muttered, 'Sure, it's too hot for me to be sleeping. I'm going over to the saloon for a beer. You want me to bring you boys back a jug of ale?'

'That's a good idea, Jim,' Sam replied. 'Don't be long. I don't want you getting drunk.'

'Oh, I never get drunk if I've got t'ings to do,' Murphy assured him, and went stomping off down the stairs.

'I still don't trust that coyote,' Frank muttered. 'There's something about him.'

Jim plodded over to the saloon, glancing furtively back at their hotel window to see if he was being watched, then changed course and made his way to the telegraph office. He leaned over the counter and asked the operator to send a telegraph to the address on the bit of paper the ranger had entrusted to him.

The old guy peered up from beneath his green eye-shade and asked, 'What you want to say, young fella?'

'We are on our way to Round Rock to rob the bank,' Murphy hissed. 'For God's sake get there.'

'What? Are you joking?'

'No, I ain't. Dis is a matter of life and death,' Murphy whispered, huskily. 'I'm working under cover for the Texas Rangers. Just send what I say and everything will be be fine and dandy.'

'Anything you say, son.' The oldster shrugged and tapped out the message. 'All telegraphs are private and confidential. That'll be fifty cents.'

'Good. Just don't breathe a word about this to nobody. Or my life won't be worth a dime.'

Clint Anderson reached Fort Worth about seven the next morning and, after rubbing down Rocky and giving him a feed, called in at the rangers' head-quarters, adjacent to the town jail.

Captain Lee Hall had his boots up on the desk and they exchanged greetings. He was a good man who had taken a prime part, along with Clint, in putting down the vicious Baker gang, and latterly in the arrest of Clay Allison.

'How's it going, Lee?' the captain asked. 'Any messages for me?'

'No, all quiet. I've been told to hold the fort.' Clint had arranged with the governor that should anything come through from Murphy he should be contacted immediately at the rangers' office. 'If you get anything for me from Dick Coke let me know immediately, Lee. And keep it under your hat. We don't want too many law 'n order men stepping in and bungling things for us.'

They passed the time of day for a bit, but Clint could hardly keep his eyes open, weary from the long night ride. He decided to go take a nap at his lodgings along the road. 'I'll be back about eleven to man the desk and give you a break,' he said.

While he was away Major J.B. Johnston galloped his horse in to the rangers' office accompanied by his crony, Chris Connor, and two other rangers, Dick Ware and George Herold. He tossed his reins to Connor to stable his mount round the back with the others and stomped noisily inside.

He was sat on the desk, chewing the fat with Lee Hall, when a telegraph boy with a message arrived. It was addressed to Captain Anderson, but J.B. said he'd handle it. He tore it open and studied the contents. 'It's from the governor. Sounds like Bass and his gang are planning a raid on the bank at Round Rock.'

'Really?' The rangy, fair-haired Lee got to his feet

and held out his hand. 'I'd better take that along to show Clint.'

'There ain't no time for that.' The major consulted his gold timepiece. Although the outlying Texan townships were mainly served by stagecoach routes, the railroads had by now established lines between major towns. 'There's a train leaving for Round Rock in twenty minutes. Go tell Chris and the boys to git tooled up. We're gonna be on it.'

Lee Hall hesitated. 'I understood Clint had been put in charge of this assignment. Maybe I've got time to go get him.'

'No! I'm your superior officer and you do what I damn well tell you, Ranger,' Johnson roared. 'We don't want that uppity young fool muscling in on this and trying to steal our glory. Every second counts. You go call in the boys.'

Lee scowled, but knew better than to argue with J.B. He chose a carbine from the rack and went to do what he was told. When he was gone the major scrawled out messages to Sheriff Andy Grimes, of Williamson County, and Sheriff Morris Moore, of Travis. 'Get to Round Rock and wait for our arrival.' He didn't deem it necessary to inform them of what exactly was happening.

'Here, boy,' he grunted out, phlegmatically, to the telegraph boy who was standing by gawping. 'Get back immediately and have these messages sent.' He found a silver dollar in his pocket and flicked it to him. 'That should cover it. Any change you can keep it.'

The major laughed heartily to himself as he checked his revolver and clacked home the cylinder. 'That idiot's gonna miss all the fun,' he chuckled. 'And the reward money.'

The rangers burst back in, excitedly, and selected carbines and ammunition. 'There's something cookin' at Round Rock,' J.B. shouted. 'We won't be needin' the hosses. We're travellin' in style. Come on, men, follow me.'

The last to leave, Lee Hall, was about to lock the door, but he went back to the desk and scribbled out, 'Round Rock. No time to warn you. You better hurry.'

SIX

It was a sweltering hot afternoon in mid-July when the Bass gang sauntered their horses into Round Rock. The town, huddled beneath the bald dome of granite that inspired its name, was peacefully quiet with only the clang of steel from the smithy, the scrape of cutlery on china in a restaurant, the clink of gaming chips and murmur of conversation from the saloon. Scrubby horses at the hitching rails fretted and flicked their tails at tormenting flies. A small group of ragged children giggled as they fought a battle with mock guns, then turned to watch the strangers pass by.

'There's the bank,' Sam muttered, as they ambled past the only building of red brick among the clapboard houses, stores and false fronts. A farmer climbed from his wagon and went inside to do business.

'He'd better hurry,' Seaborne guffawed, 'if he's gonna make a withdrawal.'

Jim Murphy licked his lips and glanced nervously about as he rode beside the surly, silent Frank Jackson, who held his Sharps carbine across the pommel of his saddle, forefinger hooked around the trigger.

Where are they? Murphy wondered. Don't say they ain't got here. What'll I do then?

He, however, like the others, was unaware they were being watched. Major James B. Johnson had been awaiting the gang's arrival for two hours, his four rangers deployed so they had the bank in their gunsights from every angle. He knelt at the window of the town hotel front bedroom, his rifle in his hands. 'Here they come,' he snorted. 'At last.'

Lee Hall, beside him, said, 'They're going on past.'

'They'll be back.' J.B. signalled with his rifle to Chris Connor, who was seated in the window of the barber shop as if awaiting a haircut. Connor touched the brim of his hat to indicate he understood, and winked at Ranger Harold.

Across the road from them, on a chair in the shade of the sidewalk canopy, Ranger Dick Ware whittled at a stick. In his crumpled range clothes he looked like any out-of-work cowboy with nothing to do. When Bass and his boys had passed he loosened the revolver in the holster beneath his coat and watched them go.

Major Johnson grunted with satisfaction. 'Murphy's with them.'

'Yeah,' Lee drawled. 'Set loose to do the Devil's work.'

Clint Anderson had roused himself from sleep at 11 a.m. that morning and strolled down to the rangers' headquarters only to find them all gone. 'I bet J.B.'s behind this,' he gritted out to himself as he saw Lee's note. 'He'll just as likely ruin everything.'

He hurried to Fort Worth railroad depot. 'When's the next train to Round Rock?' he shouted at a guard.

'There ain't one 'til tomorrow. Only thing heading there today is that goods train.' The railroadman pointed to a Puffing Billy that was clattering away along the track hauling a string of vans. 'You sure won't ever catch that.'

'Hot damn!' Clint didn't wait to argue. Holding onto his heavy revolver to steady it he ran as fast as his high-heeled boots and spurs permitted along to the livery. He didn't bother saddling Rocky, just slipped a bridle over his head, the bit into his jaws and vaulted aboard. 'Hee-yaugh!' he yelled, whipping him with the reins as he raced out of the barn doors and headed down the road in a cloud of dust.

The goods train had got a good start on him and, smoke pouring from its stack, was putting on speed. But they were heavily loaded wagons and Rocky was a match for it. Clint spurred the dun into a full gallop along the side of the track. 'Come on, boy,' he yelled. 'You can make it.'

Gradually they drew level and the ranger steadied

himself, judged the distance and hurled himself from the saddle, catching hold of an iron ladder on the side of the rear van to haul himself aboard.

He glanced back to see that Rocky had slowed and with a puzzled look on his face was watching him go. The dun would no doubt find his way back to his stall.

Clint held on tight, catching his breath as the van clanged along on the rails. He climbed to the top, peering through the grit and woodsmoke and set off towards the engine, leaping from one van to the next, at one point his boots slipping perilously, but he managed to steady himself.

'Hi,' he shouted to the engineer when he eventually jumped down to join him, showing his ranger's badge. 'Can't you get any more speed out of this thing? I'm in a hurry to get to Round Rock.'

Thus it was that as the four outlaws walked their horses down the wide main drag the locomotive finally blasted its whistle as Round Rock town's cluster of houses came into sight.

When they reached Koppel's corner store Seaborne Barnes scratched at his curly beard and beamed at them. 'Have I got time to buy me some barley sugar?'

'Sure.' Bass tore Jack Davies's letter to pieces for safety's sake and climbed from his own horse. 'There's no hurry. I wanna get the feel of the town before we hit.'

'Yeah,' Jackson drawled, jumping down. 'I wanna

get me some ceegars 'fore we head for Mexico.' He studied some coins in his hand. 'That's if I got enough cash.'

Seaborne roared with laughter and slapped his shoulder. 'Frank, I'll treat you to that. By tonight we'll be rich pigs. Enough cash in our pokes to live like kings. Beef steaks, whiskey and wimmin, that's what we'll be havin'.'

'Keep your voice down. Don't tell the whole damn town.' Sam frowned as Seaborne jumped up onto the sidewalk and swaggered into the store. So far this year they had drawn puny rewards in Texas: eleven dollars when they held up the Fort Worth coach; seventy dollars from another stage robbery in February. It was chickenfeed. Later that month they had done better when they hit the Houston and Texas central express at Allen station and raked $2,280 from the passengers. But in March when they tried again on the same line the passengers were dirt poor and the baggage car bare.

No, true, he didn't need the cash. But it was a matter of pride. Round Rock was the one Texans would remember him by.

'I don't want to start no shooting,' he muttered, edgily. 'But if anybody gets in our way it'll be their funeral.'

Murphy flicked his lank hair out of his eyes and glanced around nervously. 'Maybe I'd better go take a look along by the bank, Sam,' he stuttered. 'Make sure there's no rangers around.'

'Yeah, you do that.' Sam forced a grin. 'We'll be along in a few minutes. Don't you worry, Jim. All you gotta do is hold the hosses while we go in the bank.'

The four outlaws were unaware that Sheriffs Moore and Grimes had just arrived in town and were watching them from the doorway of a restaurant across the road. The two lawmen were still in the dark about what was going on as they didn't realize the rangers were already waiting in ambush. But they didn't like the look of these four.

A notice was clearly displayed outside the town jail that gun-toting was not allowed in Round Rock. All firearms had to be handed in during the duration of a visit. But the three characters who had disappeared into Koppel's shop were packing iron, six-guns pig-stringed to thighs like professional shootists, belts packed with bullets and one of them carrying a heavy carbine. Those dust-covered delinquents were obviously up to no good.

The fourth, more scruffily dressed one, had ambled away leading his horse back along the road. There was something bulky in his coat pocket, probably a gun.

'Let's see what they're up to,' Sheriff Moore said, leading the way across to Koppel's.

The three outlaws were passing the time of day with Mr Koppel when the two lawmen with tin stars on their shirts stepped into the store.

'You boys hold it right there,' Sheriff Grimes began to say. 'We need to tell you about them guns you're packing—'

Seaborne Barnes was just about to crunch a stick of barley sugar in his teeth. His jaw dropped and so did the candy bar. 'You mean this gun, Sheriff?' he asked, with mock astonishment, reaching for his revolver.

Suddenly bullets began to fly as Bass swung around, his Smith & Wesson already in his fist and spitting flame and death. Frank Jackson jerked up his Sharps, levering it fast and effectively from the hip. Seaborne joined in, blazing away with his Colt.

Grimes didn't even have time to get his gun out. He was catapulted back into a a crate of apples, his arms outstretched, bleeding from six bullets in his body, stone dead.

Sheriff Moore, standing behind him, managed to fire five times before a bullet ploughed into his heart, knocking him to the shop floor where he expired in a pool of blood.

It was all over in a matter of seconds. Koppel and his customers froze as the blackpowder smoke curled away to reveal the three desperadoes standing there with smoking guns.

'Hell take 'em,' Seaborne yelled. 'They asked for it. What we gonna do now, Sam? We gonna go for the bank?'

'Why not?' Sam looked about him before carefully reloading the Smith & Wesson. 'How about you, Frank? You OK?'

'Sure, not a scratch.' Jackson grinned wildly at the

other two. 'C'm on. Let's go fer it.'

Major Johnson heard the sound of gunfire and yelled, 'What in thunder's going on?'

Lee poked his head out of the hotel bedroom window and peered up the street. 'They're riding down here fast.'

'Get ready to start shootin', captain.'

Both men shouldered their weapons and watched Sam, Jackson and Barnes haul their mustangs to a halt, jump from them and tether them to a hitching rail.

'Where's Murphy?' Jackson shouted, levering his carbine. 'I never did trust that sonuvabitch.'

Sam took his own carbine from the saddle boot and nodded, grimly, to his two accomplices. 'Come on.'

They set off together across the street towards the bank. They were halfway across when Major Johnson and Captain Hall poked their rifles out the window and began shooting, joined simultaneously by Chris Connor and George Herold from the doorway of the barber shop. Ranger Dick Ware dived for cover and let loose with his revolver.

Caught in the vicious crossfire the three bandits tried to run back to their horses, but Lee Hall took careful aim and Seaborne Barnes spun in his tracks as the bullet got him. He hit the dust and lay arms and legs sprawled, blood pumping from his chest.

Frank Jackson blazed away with his powerful carbine, making the rangers duck for cover as windows were smashed. He levered it non-stop until its seven-shot magazine was empty, giving Sam a chance to leap on his wild-eyed mustang and whip it away at a gallop down the street. Bullets whistled and whined about him but he appeared to be getting away.

Jackson tossed the carbine away, drew his revolver, caught his horse and hauled himself aboard, spurring it up onto the sidewalk and sending it leaping to crash through the window of a haberdashery store. Women screamed and were tumbled aside as he rode the horse through the shop and out of the back door. He careered for two blocks then doubled his mount back along an alleyway to the main street.

Suddenly Jackson saw Murphy cowering in a doorway, a stricken look on his ill-nourished face. The older man cursed and aimed his revolver at the Irishman, snapping off a shot. He missed. 'You lousy snake in the grass,' he shouted. 'You're a dead man.' But he didn't have time to try again as the rangers were running towards him. He swung his sturdy mount around and set off in the opposite direction to which Sam had gone. Soon he would be just a speck on the plain, heading south towards Mexico.

'It sounds like they've started the party without me,' Clint cried, leaping from the steam engine as it eased into Round Rock. He set off at a run towards the noise of a gun battle. Suddenly he saw Sam Bass in his dark dusty suit come racing his mustang down the wide main street. He stood his ground and raised his Peacemaker in his right hand, arm extended, steadying his grip with his left fist. He took aim at Sam's distraught face and the revolver spat lead.

Sam returned fire and galloped straight at him, trying to run him down, but Clint jumped aside and fired again. He had the satisfaction of seeing Bass retch with pain as the bullet hit him in the chest. Then the horse had flashed past and Sam went on his way.

The ranger quickly unhitched a bronc standing at the rail, jumped into the saddle and set off in pursuit. He rode for five miles, but with his poor mount could not catch up. His horse was almost done in and blowing hard when he spotted a small ranch house up ahead. From behind a barn door a farmer was signalling to him and pointing inside. Clint jumped down, cocked his Peacemaker and took a careful look. A bullet nearly took off his ear but it was the last Sam Bass ever fired. Clint Anderson replied in kind and Sam fell back into the straw.

'You're dying, Sam,' Clint said, as he relieved him of the revolver. 'You ain't gonna last long. Why don't you tell us where the rest of the cash is?'

'I may be dying, but I ain't one to dish in my friend. Too bad, Ranger, what I know will die with me.'

The ranger knelt beside him and quickly searched him. There was nothing of much consequence, but in his coat pocket he found a stagecoach company receipt. Sam tried to snatch it, but he held it from him. 'What's this?' he muttered.

Suddenly he heard the rest of the rangers arriving outside and he tucked the receipt into his own pocket and rose to meet them.

'Two lawmen murdered,' Lee Hall blurted out. 'You were right. The major certainly made a fine cock-up of things. They should have been warned.'

'Yeah,' Clint drawled, as the red-faced Johnson blustered in, trying to shout down Captain Hall. 'I mighta known. Well, I guess the least you can do is go and inform those men's widows, J.B. And while you do so I'll claim the reward on Sam here. Howja like that!'

SEVEN

Three Fingers Jack Davis leaned on the rail of his corral and watched his three *cibeleros*, with their sharp-pointed lances, on their fiery mustangs, chasing his six young bulls. They were good and ready. It was time to take them into Zaragoza to sell. 'Bring 'em out,' he shouted in Spanish. 'I'll follow you along.'

Jack had done well since arriving in Mexico ten months before with $15,000 in gold in his pack-bags. He had picked up this fortified *hacienda* and thirty miles of scrub range stretching back up a secluded valley for $1,000, a mere bagatelle. It was going cheap because the owner had died and due to its remote location fifty miles from the nearest main town. Protecting its back was the Serenias de Burro, a picturesque chain of mountains, one snow-tipped peak reaching nearly 3,000 feet into the blue sky.

Living, like life, itself, was cheap in Mexico, and pleasant if a man belonged to the ruling landowner class. Sure, he was at the base of the pyramid which kept dictator Porfirio Diaz in power. Some *estancias* stretched for 500 miles, and the generals at the top, and the Roman Catholic church, which had been reinstated with vast land grants, commanded undreamed of wealth.

However, Three Fingers Jack – or Señor Jack Artemio, as he was now known – was pleased with his lot. His half-dozen *vaqueros*, whom he had chosen for their ability with horse and gun, were happy with a pittance, by American standards, as long as they had enough to go out at the end of each month to get almighty drunk. His house servants, grooms and a handful of *peons* who toiled in his fields he paid even less. Altogether, from the sale of cattle for slaughter, and these wild fighting bulls, he looked to make a good profit on his lay-out this first year, and even more the next.

His house lay back behind high protective walls and was itself lofty, cool and spacious. It had been built as a defence against Apache attacks, but the day of the Apache warrior was fast coming to an end, even if Geronimo's small band were still leading American troopers a merry dance north of the border.

'Hey, Teresa,' Davis roared, as he stepped into his hallway. 'Hurry it up and make sure you're looking your best. We're going to meet the governor.'

This was met by a volley of Spanish from a stocky, middle-aged lady in black silk, who came from a bedroom to the top of the stairs. She was Maria, the maid and *duenna*, as they called them, of his young mistress Teresa, whose job was to escort her at all times to keep an eye on her virtue.

The gist of her shrill lament was how could she ever get this rebellious, mischievous child ready to go anywhere on time. 'Tell her I'll be up there with my bullwhip to scorch her backside if she don't behave herself and get a move on,' Jack bellowed.

It was no idle threat, as Teresa resentfully acknowledged from bitter experience. Three Fingers Jack figured that a touch of the lash was the best tonic to keep cows, horses, *peons*, dogs and feisty gals in line. Indeed, he often drunkenly enjoyed giving his young charge a sadistic teasing with his whip before having his way with her. Of course, he was always careful not to scar her pretty face. All had gone quiet up in the bedroom so she was probably pulling a sulky look as she allowed herself to be dressed in the height of Mexican fashion.

Jack unlocked a small room off the big central banqueting hall, which he used as his office, and then opened a huge iron safe. He took out only a handful of gold coins and slid them into his pocket. He wouldn't need more because he would be paid in gold for the bulls once he reached Zaragoza. He had already sold some to the ring there, donating one free to the people of the town to ensure their friendship. His bulls, with their deadly horns, had proved brave and popular as they fought. In fact, Jack had cultivated the bullring impresarios and had already had several offers to provide his bulls to other rings. He was currently negotiating for the big prize, Mexico City.

'For God's sake get a move on,' he shouted as he went out to make sure their open landau, a smart two-horse rig, and their protective outriders were good and ready for the fifty-mile trip to the market town. They would take their ease, breaking the journey with an overnight stay at the village of Rosita *en route*.

Teresa appeared, looking a picture in a dress of crimson lace over black silk, primped and powdered, her shiny dark hair combed up in an ornate arrangement beneath her mantilla, and carrying a parasol. One of the coachmen gulped lustfully as he watched her step up into the landau in the process displaying shapely calves in silk stockings and silver high-heeled shoes.

'I hate getting dressed-up like this in the middle of the morning,' she moaned, as she settled herself in a corner. 'It's such a bore.'

'You're my gal and the *peons* want to see you in all your splendour as we pass by. They don't get much of a treat from their labours, do they? Let 'em know we're people of importance in the state of Coahuila, that's my motto.'

'I feel like a stuffed doll,' Teresa pouted. 'It's so hot. Can't we have the cover up for shade?'

'If you don't shut up you *will* be a stuffed doll,'

Jack growled. 'I'll kick you out and leave you sittin' on your ass in the dust. What you whining about? Ain't you ever grateful for all I've done for you?'

'What, stealing me from my home, my family, my parents, raping me, keeping me here as your whore?'

'I didn't steal you. I paid 'em well and they was glad of the cash.'

He grumpily settled back into his own corner, roaring, 'C'mon. Get this rig on the road. What you waitin' for?' As they set off out from the house and along the winding track through the rocky valley, he muttered, 'No, you can't have the cover up .How they gonna see us if we do that?'

'What, not even if it pours?' Teresa sparkily replied, giving a little smile at the *duenna* to signify scoring a point.

'That's different,' Jack groaned. 'Wimmin! Why do you always have to argue?'

He, himself, was attired in clean linen and loose bowtie, the trousers of his suit tucked into riding boots. His one allowance to Mexican custom was the big sombrero. He carried a heavy converted Dragoon six-gun in the hoster of his cartridge belt and his muddy eyes brooded malevolently. She had deliberately put him into a bad mood. If Teresa wasn't careful she would taste the whip again tonight, then she wouldn't sit down so comfortably.

For reassurance, his heel touched the small iron-bound trunk beneath his seat in which he carried his business papers and the jewellery, the necklace of rubies set in gold, and matching bracelet and ear-rings. Worth a pretty penny. Teresa would wear them at the bullfight as guest of honour in the impresarios' box and at the governor's ball. That would let 'em all know what a man of substance he was.

Consequently, he kept an eye cocked for trouble. There might not be Apaches, but there were bandits and highway robbers aplenty in this state. It was always wise to travel well-armed.

At Rosita they were greeted by the town mayor, an ingratiating shopkeeper Jack did business with. But the accommodations and supper he offered in his home was fine enough. Feeling magnaminous, Jack allowed Teresa to go visit her family, who lived nearby, on condition she returned by nine o'clock.

Over supper the mayor's straight-laced wife eyed the girl curiously. She had expected better of Teresa, who had always seemed an honest, upright girl. Why had she chosen to be the plaything of this rough, if rich American *hombre*, Señor Jack? Ah, well, many an innocent had stepped onto the slippery slope into hellfire and eternal damnation tempted by the glint of gold. Or had the poor creature been pushed? Teresa had three sisters younger than her. What were her parents to do but try to find them wealthy husbands? She had certainly flowered into a graceful young *señorita* who would catch admiring glances from any man. But why did the Americano not marry her, save her soul? It was the least he could do. 'He is unworthy of her,' she whispered to herself. 'I must pray for her.'

Much to Three Fingers Jack's relief, Teresa behaved herself admirably at the bullfight, was presented with the ears and tail by a matador, and in her finery and rubies was the talk of the town in Zaragoza, quite the sparkling belle of the governor's ball. Jack, too, did good business and made valuable contacts and was well pleased.

'You see,' he told her that night, as he pulled off his boots sitting on the bed in a guest suite of the governor's palace, 'you behave properly, gal, an' I might not have to be so strict with you. You can do it, you see.'

Sitting at the dressing-table, removing her jewellery, her dress, Teresa did not reply. What was this leading up to? What foul demands would he make of her tonight? The touch of his deformed hand made her flesh crawl.

News of Sam Bass's death travelled fast in Texas. Even before the state governor had given a statement to the *Fort Worth Pioneer* and other news sheets, it was on everybody's lips. Major James B. Johnson tried to claim credit for the ambush, but Governor Coke quickly quashed that idea when eye-witnesses testified they had seen Captain Anderson fire the first of two fatal shots. They dug the slugs from Sam's body to check. Sure enough, they were from a Colt Peacemaker .45, not the Winchester .44 carbines the other rangers had used.

'The heinous slaughter of two brave peace officers, Sheriff Moore and Sheriff Grimes, by Bass and
his two fellow partners-in-crime has been avenged.
Our rangers undoubtedly showed great courage, but
it was Captain Clinton Anderson who set up the
scene and lured the outlaws into a trap. Therefore I
have no hesitation in recommending that he be
granted the substantial reward,' were Coke's words.
'Captain Anderson has privately informed me that
he will be donating a thousand dollars of this to his
fellow rangers, and a thousand dollars to the fund I
have set up for the widows and families of the
murdered peace officers.'

While amused at putting J.B.'s nose out-of-joint,
Clint Anderson was not happy to see his picture plas-
tered on the front pages, nor that his words in private
to Coke had been released. But he gritted his teeth
and ignored Major Johnson's taunts as J.B. read out
aloud *The Pioneer.*

'Look at the picture of the hero. Don't he try to
paint himself whiter than white.' he said.

To most of the rangers gathered at their head-
quarters at Fort Worth this sounded like sour grapes.
Indeed, the four apart from J.B., who took part in the
ambush at Round Rock were glad to get something
for putting their lives on the line. A formal enquiry
had been held into what went wrong and, after hearing testimony, Governor Coke put the blame for the
deaths of the peace officers squarely on the shoulders of Major Johnson. 'You took it upon yourself to

set the ambush in operation without informing them who we were after, or even that these criminals would be armed and dangerous. Nor did you notify Captain Anderson of events as I had instructed you should. You just went charging off like a bull in a china shop. For this reason I am seriously inclined to ask you to resign from the Rangers, Major.'

J.B. jumped to his feet to protest, vehemently. 'You can't do that! I'm a war veteran. I fought with Forrest. If it weren't for me and my frontier battalion protecting Texas from Comanches you wouldn't be sitting here safe and snug in your armchair today, Coke.'

'That's enough,' Dick Coke snapped. 'You're too big for your boots, J.B., and too damn old. I'm not only taking you off active duty, I'm asking you to hand in your badge.'

'Just a minute, Governor.' Anderson rose to his feet and spread his hands, trying to calm them. 'That's a bit harsh. I ain't an admirer of the major's methods, and in my opinion he's a hothead, but he's done long and almost legendary service for this state.'

'I don't need you to speak for me,' J.B. butted in. 'You—'

Clint ignored him and added, 'I suggest you confine him to frontier fighting from here on.'

'Right.' The governor frowned, malevolently, at the major. 'You just hold your tongue, Johnson, or you'll be outa here. But I think the captain's made a wise suggestion, so you can stay in the force. Just watch your step, you hear?'

'Well, he *was* my father-in-law,' Clint muttered to Lee Hall. 'I spoke up for Mary's sake.'

The governor had gone on to other business. 'It appears there's still probably thirty thousand missing in stolen money in the area south of the Red River. Frank Jackson and Three Fingers Jack are still on the loose. What are you boys gonna do about it? Any ideas, Clint?'

'Yep.' Anderson rose to his feet again. 'I've seen evidence pointing to the possible whereabouts of Three Fingers Jack. But I'd prefer to keep my cards close to my chest. I guess you understand why, Governor.'

Johnson got up and bellowed, 'Is he suggesting I'm not to be trusted? I've never heard of—'

'Shut your mouth, J.B.,' Coke shouted. 'He ain't mentioned you by name, but if the cap fits wear it.'

'I was going to say I'd like permission to go after Davis into Mexico,' Clint added. 'I'd prefer to act on my own, incognito.'

'We couldn't give you any authority to act as a Texas Ranger across the border,' Coke replied. 'We got enough problems with the Mexican Government as it is. But if you think you've got a chance of bringing back some of this cash you're free to give it a try.'

Clint shrugged and drawled, 'Good. In that case, I guess I'd better be on my way.'

As the meeting broke up Governor Dick Coke

went over to Clint and stuck out his hand. 'Good luck, Captain. You don't need me to tell you to watch your back.'

'There's one thing.' Clint scratched his jaw. 'When do I get paid the reward on Sam?'

'You'll get it, don't you worry,' the governor said. 'But you know how it is: I have to get the approval of the others who put up the reward money. It has to go through committee. These things take time. The good news is, if you bring back Three Fingers Jack there's five thousand on his head, too. You'll be a wealthy man, Ranger.'

'Yeah, maybe,' Anderson muttered. 'If I'm not a dead one.'

'Why should he get all the chances of cash and glory?' Major Johnson demanded of his crony, Chris Connor. 'It ain't right. Why don't we get the chance to go?'

'What, go down to Mexico alone?' Connor said. 'He's welcome to it. He must be crazy as a loon to volunteer. He'll have no back-up down there. Come on, Major, let's go get a drink. All this jabber makes my head spin.'

'I still don't like it. That creep gets all the breaks. He knows something we don't know.'

'Aw, come on, J.B., he saved your hide, didn't he? If it hadn't been for Anderson speaking up you'd have been forcibly retired. He ain't so bad. I don't understand this grudge you got against him.'

'If it had been your daughter those savages got,'

the major growled, 'you'd sure understand.'

When Jim Murphy arrived back in Denton they certainly didn't get the town band out to greet him. Even though the governor had promised his name would be kept quiet somebody had leaked the facts to *The Pioneer* and Jim was publicly fingered as the 'cowardly rat' who betrayed his friends. They had even started to sing a song about him in the saloons. Folks in the stores, settlers loading wagons in the street, stood in their tracks to stare at him as he ambled along the sidewalk. When he stepped into Ryan's bar all the customers stopped whatever they were doing. There was a fraught silence you could have cut with a knife. To make matters worse he had yet to be paid any reward so he couldn't buy the friendship of his erstwhile drinking cronies. 'Hiya, boys,' he croaked out. But the men at the bar moved away to their separate ends as if he might contaminate them. They muttered in groups among themselves and cast looks his way that made his blood run cold.

'I'd watch your back if I were you,' the sheriff told him. 'Sam Bass was a popular boy.'

To save himself hundreds of miles of riding, Clint Anderson put Rocky in a goods van and travelled south on the railroad from Fort Worth to the terminus at San Antonio. He booked into the town hotel overlooking the busy market square, checked his guns and ammunition, bought some basic supplies which he packed into his saddle-bags, and wandered off to buy a meal and a beer. He returned to the hotel early intending to get a good night's rest before setting off for Eagle Pass.

'Howdy,' she whispered, huskily, as he stepped into the room. Kathleen was sitting on the bed, her back against the wall, and her crisp white skirts rustled invitingly as she pulled up one knee and gave him a dazzling smile. 'How ya doing, cowboy? We meet again.'

'What the hell!' Clint swallowed his surprise. 'Where's your husband?'

'George? Oh, he's miles away, at our new oil well in Bay Town. That's near Galveston.'

'Yes, I know that. But what are you doing here?'

'They told me at Fort Worth where you were headed, so I followed. I like train journeys. Don't worry about George. He's not the jealous sort.'

Clint locked the door and tossed his hat away, running fingers through his thick hair. He sat on the bed beside her. 'This ain't right, Kathleen.'

'I know it ain't.' Her cold green jewels of eyes met his and she gently stroked his shoulder through the wool shirt. 'I had to see you again. I couldn't let you just go off.'

This was foolishly risky. It had no future. It was against his code and he knew it could turn bad. Never trust a woman – the thought occurred to him for some reason. But he could not help himself. It was as if they were drawn to each other by some inner magnet, she hypnotized him, as if they were jointly burned by some fire in their veins. This time he did not tell her to undress. He pushed her down onto the bed, a surge of desire in him impossible to resist. He was kissing her succulent cherry-red lips, the forbidden fruit of life he had to bite into, to taste and, as she willingly opened to him, he tore her underskirts apart and thrust himself into her.

'Whoo!' he gasped, as some while later he lay back with her in his arms. 'What you do to a man!'

'I could do it every day, Clint,' she murmured. 'When you get back.'

This statement silenced him for a bit and he listened to the sounds out in the street, voices, a woman's laughter, someone singing a Spanish lament. 'I don't get you,' he said.

'Of course you do.' She sprang up to kneel over him, her warm, bare breasts spilling over his chest. 'We'll run away together, darling. We'll go to Wyoming. You were saying there's land and good grass up there for the taking now the Sioux have been subdued. We'll have our own ranch.'

'Hang on a minute, Kathleen. You're a woman with a wealthy husband, used to the luxuries of life. I somehow cain't see you as a rancher's woman. It's a hard, bleak life.'

'No, it wouldn't have to be. You'd be wealthy, too, once you get these rewards. We could have servants, the best.'

'I ain't got no rewards yet. I'm just a wandering saddle tramp chasing his dream. I can't guarantee—'

'And another thing,' she interrupted. 'I read you promised to give two thousand dollars away to the rangers and those widows. Don't you think that was a rather stupid thing to do? You're too idealistic, Clint. You've got to hang on to all you can get. We'll never be rich if you behave like that.'

He watched the moonlight and shadows in the room playing upon her pale naked body, gleaming on her blonde hair and shining eyes. 'Gittin' as rich as Shanghai Pierce ain't my dream. I just wanna make myself a decent life.'

'I know that, honey. But what if you recover all that cash Sam Bass and Jack Davis stole, you're surely not thinking of giving it back?'

'Sure I am. It belongs to the New York bank. They've offered a ten per-cent share. That would be a tidy sum.'

'Yes.' She pouted her ruddy lips. 'I suppose it's better than nothing. I guess we could manage.'

'Come on, Kathleen. Don't go countin' your chickens before they're hatched. There's a strong possibility all I'll get for my trouble is a bullet in the guts.'

'Don't be silly.' She smothered him with kisses, then murmured, 'You can do it, darling, and you'll bring my jewellery back. All you have to do is send me a cable and I'll be waiting for you here.'

'I ain't so sure about that,' he muttered, before

surrendering to her blandishments and rolling her over on her back again. How did I get into this? he wondered. Seems like I'm biting off more than I can chew!

EIGHT

'You got a delivery for me?' Jack Davis demanded as he strode into the stage depot at the border town of Piedras Negras. 'My name's Artemio.'

'Señor Jack Artemio?' The clerk looked up from his desk and pointed with his quill pen at a box standing in the corner of the adobe room. 'It come all way from north Texas. It been waiting here for you for two weeks.'

'Good.' Davis signed the chit, pulled out his skinning knife, and pried one of the boards from the box. He thrust a three-fingered hand into the straw and found a small canvas sack. He shook it and heard the clink of gold. There were other small sacks of coin thrust into various crevices. 'Just what I need, a new plough share,' he growled, hammering the box tight again. 'They've even sent spare washers. Very efficient stage company you run, *amigo.*'

Zaragoza was only about thirty miles from Piedras Negras and the Rio Grande – which the Mexicans knew as the Rio Bravo del Norte – and he had bade Teresa wait for him while he made the trip. He drove the two-horse landau himself and had taken along four of his wild, gun-toting *vaqueros* for protection.

Davis went outside and called to Raoul and Jaime to help him load the box onto the landau. 'Heavy, ain't it?' he grunted. 'New plough share. This should make the work of my *peons* a little easier.'

He had no wish to arouse their suspicions as to the true contents for he trusted no man. His heart pounded harder at the gleeful thought of adding to his gold reserves. He could hardly wait to count it. 'Come on, let's hit the trail. We can be back by night-fall.'

Well, the stolen gold wouldn't be any good to Sam now. It had been front page news in the Mexican journals that the notorious 'outlaw *Americano*' had cashed in his chips. Not that Jack had ever intended to give it back to Sam. Wasn't he, Jack, the one who had been the brains behind the big Central Pacific train robbery, the one who had done all the work bribing the railroad clerk in Omaha to let him know when a big consignment from the west was due. Sam was just a hick ranch hand who had gotten lucky – for a while. If he had had any sense he would have got out of Texas months ago. No, he had to try to prove how clever he was all on his own. That he had willingly agreed to send his gold down to Jack by coach proved what a stupid sucker he was.

These satisfying thoughts occurred to Three

Fingers Jack as he sent his bull-whip snaking along the backs of the two greys; his *vaqueros* loped their mustangs alongside and they ate up the miles of the trail winding across the land to Zaragoza.

'Soon I'll be top of the damn dungheap down here,' Jack snarled. 'Nobody'll be able to touch me.'

Zaragoza erupted with a loud and spectacular firework display as Ranger Clint Anderson rode in. The central square was thronged with a motley collection of people, mainly *peons* who had come in from the countryside for fiesta and, after the bullfight, the governor's ball, and prolonged church services, when religious icons had been carried through the streets, were now busy getting blind drunk on mescal and home-brewed beer.

The raucous noise of a street band, trumpets screeching, battered drums being vigorously banged, fire crackers, shrill screams and piercing whistles contended with the solemn tolling of the cathedral bells. A crazed *vaquero* appeared to have liberally dosed himself and his mustang with tequila for he was whirling the poor creature around and around amid the dancing peasants.

'What's all the hullabaloo about?'

Clint had hitched Rocky to a rail and stepped up onto the terrace of a cantina where the more well-to-do Mexicans of the town were enjoying sugary drinks and delicacies and watching the proceedings.

In their forefront was an obvious American, a

gunbelt slung around his considerable girth, his shirt patched with sweat, his spurred boots stuck out, and a flat-crowned hat perched on his bald head as he sat at a table and sipped at a murky liquid in a glass.

'Aw, how should I know?' The stranger gave a hearty guffaw and beamed at him. 'They're celebrating some saint or other. Been at it all week. Any excuse to git pie-eyed.'

'They certainly seem to know how to do that.' Clint took a spare chair at the table. 'Obliterated is more the word. Mind if I join you?'

'Looks like you already have. Make yourself at home, mister.' The fat-gutted fellow stuck out a hefty paw. 'Wilf Stringer's the handle.'

'Clint Andrews.' The tall young Texan had no wish to reveal he was a ranger. It was possible his name might have appeared in the news sheets down here if they carried reports of Sam Bass's demise, so he adopted a mild alias. 'What's that you're drinking?'

'The most evil concoction known to man. Cactus juice. Some call it mescal.' Stringer pushed the bottle across. 'Spin your brains, mister.'

'No, thanks.' Clint wanted to keep a clear head, and signalled to a Mex waiter. 'I'll stick to beer.'

He had an idea he had seen the fat man's mugshot someplace, but that was not unlikely. Most *Americanos* south of the border were drifters on the lam. Not that that bothered him. He was after bigger fish. Wilf Stringer looked like he knew how to use the shotgun propped against his chair and the shooting iron slung under his belly. He might come in useful. The ranger could well be in need of some back-up for what he was planning.

First, Anderson relaxed and took a draught of his beer to wash away the dust of the 300-mile ride from his throat. Five hot days and nights in the saddle pushing the stout-hearted Rocky on through Eagle Pass and down to the border to ford the Rio Grande. The receipt taken from the dying Sam Bass had indicated some sort of parcel dispatched to Piedras Negras.

'You're too late, mister,' the clerk in the office told him. 'Some *hombre* picked it up the day before yesterday. No, how do I know where he come from? All I know is he headed back to Zaragoza.'

The Mexican clerk had become more amenable when the ranger slapped a silver dollar into his greasy palm. 'His name? Sure, I got it here somewhere. Señor Jack Artemio. Why you interested? What's so special about plough shares?'

'You'd be surprised.' In spite of his weariness, Clint had clambered back on Rocky and headed on his way. He hadn't had much sleep the past few days, but he had an idea what that consignment to Señor Jack might have contained.

Now he sat and watched the *peons* as they forgot the hard toil of their lives for a day or three. 'Mexico sure don't change much, does it?' he said, as goatskins of alcohol were spilled down throats, sixguns fired wildly into the air.

'What would Mexico be without churches and whores, guitars and guns?' Stringer beamed expansively. 'It suits me.'

'What brings you this way, Wilf?'

'Me?' Stringer gave a caustic guffaw and wiped away perspiration that trickled from the creases of his double chin. 'I got my guns for hire. I go where I get paid best. First it was fighting for li'l Benito. When he kicked the bucket I altered my allegiance to Diaz and his thugs. But he's got his *rurales*, the scum of the prisons. He don't need me. Still,' he shrugged, spreading his hands, 'I like it down here.'

'You mean you can't go back? No offence, pal, that don't interest me. Maybe you could work for me. You heard of a guy called Jack Davis, or Artemio?'

'Maybe I have.' Stringer rolled his eyes, saucily. 'Maybe I haven't.'

'Don't play hard to get. There's a hundred dollars in it if you guide me to him.'

'A hundred? You joking? What you think I am, some messenger boy? If you're looking for Three Fingers Jack you're looking for trouble, boy. Trouble costs money where I come from. I wouldn't budge from this chair for less than two thousand.'

'So you know him?'

'Sure I know him. He was sitting in the bigwigs' box at the bullfight three days ago. I tell you, pal, I couldn't take my eyes off that li'l *señorita* of his, pretty as a picture she was, all titivated up in one of them low-cut frilly dresses of ther'n, gold flashing around her neck and wrist, dangling from her sweet li'l ears.'

'A gold necklace. Set with rubies, by any chance?'

'Yeah, you shoulda seen the blood-red glow of them big stones. That's what caught my eye in the first place. How much, I wondered, could them rubies be worth, and where had a man like Jack Artemio got 'em from in the first place?'

'Your guess is as good as mine,' Clint muttered, lowering his voice. 'Is he still in town?'

Stringer grinned, mischievously. 'You offer me a hundred greenbacks? You've had a hundred's worth of information already.'

'OK, five hundred.'

'It seems you've got an account to settle with Jack. My guess is it could mean you're interested in his cash. You can have my services to relieve him of it for half of whatever we get. I can tell you for free it won't be easy.'

'I can't make it half: it's not mine to give. Let's say I'm being paid to collect a debt. But, OK, I'll pay you a thousand, Wilf. That's a generous offer.'

'No, it ain't, that *hombre*'s snug as a bug in a rug with his li'l damsel in a high-walled hacienda fifty miles from here. It's guarded by a clutch of sharp-shooting *vaqueros*. It's virtually impregnable. We wouldn't have a snowball's chance in hell.'

'We might if we took 'em by surprise and went in shooting. Come on, Wilf. We can do it. My final offer is two thousand dollars.'

'That's better,' Wilf grunted. 'Maybe—'

'So, I asked you, are they still in Zaragoza?'

Stringer tipped back his tumbler of cloudy mescal and grinned widely, showing gappy teeth. 'So happens I saw 'em this morning, heading home.'

Anderson took a roll of greenbacks from his shirt pocket and peeled off a hundred dollars, pushing them across the table. 'That's for the information.' He stood up and said, 'I'm on my way, pal.'

'Hang on,' Wilf Stringer called. 'Count me in. When do I get paid the full amount?'

Clint smiled at him and slapped his Peacemaker. 'When we collect.'

'Yee-ha!' The morose countenance of Three Fingers Jack lit up as he punched the air. 'Allelujah!'

Locked away in his office, he had just finished counting the piles of sparkling gold cartwheels: $12,500, Sam's bounty was more than he could have hoped for. He carefully began stacking it away with the $13,000 of his own cash left from the train robbery after buying the house, land and stock. Things were looking rosy.

'Maybe I didn't oughta keep all of my eggs in one basket,' he muttered to himself, not immune to a miser's fear of robbery. But he didn't trust banks, certainly not Mexican ones. 'Maybe I oughta dig a few hidey-holes up in the hills and disperse this little lot.'

Tomorrow he would think about that. Today he would be busy getting the *cibeleros* to bring in the last of his fighting bulls. It was the height of the bull-fighting season and he had had an urgent request from the owner of the ring in Durango for more of them. In fact his trip to Zaragoza had been highly successful. The state governor himself, after dancing with Teresa, had told him that Americans were welcome in Mexico, mining engineers, railroadmen, cattle entrepreneurs, if they had cash to invest and the talents to go with it. If Jack would report any signs of banditry or infiltration by rebel bands into the rugged lands north-west of Jack's land to the border, he could count on the support of the *rurales* and, indeed, the gratitude of *el presidente*.

Jack locked the safe, hid the key, let himself out of his office, secured that door and turned to greet Teresa, who was coming downstairs in her morning dress. A *señorita* of her standing in society would be expected to change her dress at least three times a day. At least, this is what Maria drummed into her as she made her black hair gleam with 150 strokes of the brush. 'A girl must keep her man happy,' she told her constantly.

'Hiya, honey,' Jack shouted. 'The Lord Almighty smiles upon me. Gold, wine, bulls and a beautiful girl! What more could a man ask?'

'You're full of the joys of spring today,' Teresa replied with a downturned grimace of her pert lips. 'We're going out for a drive later on. I'm tired of being cooped up in this prison. I need some fresh air.'

'Sure, sweetheart. You go up the valley you should be safe enough. Tell Manolo and Jorge to get the rig ready. Don't step on any snakes and watch out for the bulls.' He slapped her backside as she passed and hugged her into him. 'I'm gonna be in a loving mood tonight.'

'Really?' She turned her face away with distaste as he tried to kiss her. 'I can't wait.'

They had camped the first night outside the town of Rosita. Wilf had wanted to ride in to visit the cantina, from the doorway of which a couple of painted ladies had given them lingering looks as they passed.

'No way,' Anderson said. 'Get some shuteye. We're moving out 'fore dawn.'

'What's the matter, man? Don't you like wimmin?'

'I don't particilarly want a dose of what the Comanche call a cold between the legs. Anyway, I got a woman.' The memory returned to him of Kathleen warm and naked in his arms. Could she really want to leave her rich husband, her elevated position in society, to go off with him? 'She's headache enough.'

'Oh, yeah, why?' Stringer asked, as he had rolled over in his blanket beside their fire and taken a swig of mescal.

'She's married, that's why.'

'Forget her, pal. No use pining for a dame like her. She'll be snuggling up to her hubby right now. She's just using you.' It sounded as if Stringer was speaking from bitter experience. 'Once an adulteress, always an adulteress. You take her on, pal, in a coupla years she'll be doin' the same thing to you.'

Clint made no reply, but Wilf's words drilled into his mind. Kathleen had told him she had been raised on a Louisiana plantation in the lap of luxury. But the war had ruined everything: her brothers killed at Shiloh; the house burned to the ground; her mother dead of a broken heart. Her father, a slaver, had lost all. He had taken her to New Orleans, become a cotton broker. It was there she had met George Piper, older than her, but sophisticated and wealthy. Her father had urged her to marry him. It all sounded a bit too neat. How much of it, he wondered, was true?

'Cheer up, cowboy,' Stringer said, seeing his morose face and pulling out a well-thumbed pack of cards. 'How about a little game of poker before we grab some shut-eye. Or is gambling another vice you don't approve of?'

'I'm not that much of a puritan,' Clint grinned. 'I'll risk a dollar or two. Deal me in.'

'Toss another log on the fire,' Wilf said, settling back to study his cards. 'This game could last a while.'

Three hours later, about midnight, Clint looked at his hand and gave an involuntary shudder. 'God!' he exclaimed. 'Everything's gone wrong on this assignment. Now this.'

'You look like you've seen a ghost. What's wrong?'

Clint showed his cards, a pair of aces and a pair of eights. 'Dead Man's hand!'

Wilf, too, looked momentarily taken aback. Most poker players knew it was the hand Wild Bill Hickok held when he was shot in the back in Deadwood two years before.

'The hand of misfortune for you, pal. You lose. That's fifty-three bucks you owe me.'

The ranger paid him out. 'Get some sleep.'

It was just crazy superstition, he knew, but as he rested back against his saddle he couldn't dispel a premonition of tragedy fast approaching.

With the dawn they pressed on, leaving the valley trail and climbing their horses up along the lower slopes of the rugged *cordilleras*. It was hard going and the ranger took it carefully. If Rocky took a tumble it might prove fatal for both of them because he had dynamite in his saddle-bags. However, their efforts paid off, for by high noon they found themselves standing on a bluff looking down on the fortified ranch house.

'There's a sentry with a rifle in that tower,' Clint murmured, training his pocket telescope on their target, careful to stay in the shade of a big rock so the sun's glint would not give them away. 'Two more above the main gate. Any unwelcome visitors from town can be assured of a hot reception. Maybe we could get in the back way.'

'Whichever,' Stringer grunted, 'it'll be suicidal

trying to breech them walls. We'd better wait 'til dark.'

'You've got a point.' In the clear air of the high country they could see storms blowing their back-trails across the northern plateau. It was the start of the rainy season, the blessing, as the Mexicans called it. There might be downpours to the north but here they were untouched by them, in bright sunshine. The threat of storms, however, made him eager to get this business attended to one way or the other. Clint stroked his jaw as he put the telescope aside and squatted down, waiting, watching. 'Hey,' he hissed, 'there's riders coming.'

A bunch of *vaqueros* on spirited mustangs were bringing in a knot of black bulls, giving shrill yells, cracking whips, brandishing lances. The lithe bulls ran nimbly before them, ears pricked, a threat in the poise of their strong shoulders, their sharp horns. Fierce as they might be they were no match for the ingenuity of man, and the *cibileros* ran them with apparent ease around the side of the high walls which shielded the hacienda and through the tall oak gates as they were swung open.

'There was seven of 'em,' Wilf said. 'The two on the gate, the one in the tower, that makes nine men so far.'

'Don't forget Three FIngers Jack. Hey, look, there's a coach coming out. Well, I'll be jiggered! There's two fellas on the box and two dames in the back. Where are they off to?'

Wilf snatched the telescope from him and put an eye to it. The landau, pulled by two dappled greys, was heading back up the valley, following the winding stream. A man in a sombrero held the reins while another beside him toted a shotgun. Wilf turned his attention to the two females. 'It's the li'l chickadee,' he drawled, with an expression of awe. 'Jack's girl. T'other's some tubby ol' henbird.'

Clint watched as the open landau went clipping along for half a mile, then entered a grove of willows and disappeared from sight. 'Come on,' he said. 'Let's see what they're up to while them other fellows are busy with their bulls.'

They swung onto their broncs and went charging down through a scree of dust and rocks and out at a gallop across the sun-dried grass of the valley. They reached the wood of willows, hopefully without being seen, and pulled their mounts in to tread more cautiously.

Once through the wood they could see the dust kicked up by the greys half a mile away still, so went after them. 'Where they got to?' Clint muttered, as they climbed a slight incline following a bend in the trail. 'Hold it!' He slid, instinctively, from the saddle and pulled Rocky into cover. 'There they are.'

'What they up to?' Wilf asked, huskily, as he joined him.

'Dunno. Let's take a look.' They loose-hitched their horses to rocks and climbed up over the hill, getting down on their bellies and crawling forward through the rock and scrub. But it so happened the guards had their backs to them. They were too busy watching Teresa who had taken off her stockings, tucked her skirts up around her waist, and was paddling up to her bare knees in the clear stream. She gave a squeal of mischief as she bent down to splash handfuls of water back at the portly *duenna*, Maria, who was watching her.

It was a pleasant sight, the slim, shapely girl laughing as she stood in the sun-sparkling water. A shame to interrupt, really, Clint thought, as he unholstered his Peacemaker. He stood and approached closer, Wilf alongside him, shotgun at the ready. The girl saw them first as she turned and her smile disappeared. She didn't speak as she met Anderson's eyes, just stared at him.

'Howdy,' he called, and rapped out in Spanish, 'Don't make a move.'

Jorge, the driver, was still sitting on the box. His right hand went towards the pistol on his hip, but he paused. Manolo, straddling a rock, had his shotgun in his grip. He froze, then slowly began to swivel round to take a look at them.

'Make another move it'll be the last thing you do,' Wilf barked out in frontier Spanish. 'Toss that gun away, pronto.'

For seconds it seemed both men might make a fight for it. They were at a disadvantage but there was no accounting for Mexican pride and machismo. They might prefer to go down shooting rather than suffer the shame of surrender. The sound of guns, warning those along at the hacienda, was the last thing Anderson wanted. Fortunately, these two saw sense. Manolo threw away the twelve gauge, and Jorge was persuaded to carefully remove his revolver and do likewise.

'Good thinkin', boys,' Wilf shouted, stepping up close. 'You get to fight another day.'

But the black-clothed Maria wasn't in such an amenable mood. 'How dare you?' she screeched and whacked Stringer on his head with her parasol.

'You old haybag,' he roared, as his hat was knocked sideways and she continued belabouring him. 'Quit your squawking, will ya? We ain't gonna hurt ya.'

'Rape!' the *duenna* screamed, as he caught hold of her arm, twisted her into him and put a sweaty hand across her mouth.

'Help!' she gurgled.

The sight of the *duenna* being manhandled made Teresa smile. 'Go on,' she called .'Pull her skirt up and give her bottom a good smacking!'

'Yeah, I might just give her more than that.'

Wilf struggled to constrain the tubby armful and, at the same time, keep his shotgun cocked at the two Mexicans. 'Ouch! She bit me."

Wilf pulled back his hand and gave her a hefty clout to the jaw sending her splashing backwards into the stream where she sat moaning and crossing herself, obviously awaiting a fate worse than death.

'Aw, pipe down, woman.' Clint grinned at the girl, as if seeing her immediately as an ally. 'I gather you two ain't pals.'

'No, the bossy old cow. Serves her right.' Teresa spoke shrilly to the woman to hold her tongue, then asked Anderson, 'Who are you? What do you want.'

'Whoever they are,' Jorge growled, 'they are already dead men. Señor Jack will see to that.'

'He can try,' Clint replied, and said to the girl, 'Don't worry, you won't be harmed as long as you do as I say.'

'I'm not worried,' she replied, insouciantly. 'Nor do I mind what you do to him. Please, *señor*, I am his prisoner. Take me away from here.'

'You are a shamed hussy,' Maria snapped, as she clambered from the stream in her wet dress. 'What decent man would have you now? All you're fit for is the brothel.'

'*Miaouw!*' Wilf beamed. 'Now then, girls, we're too busy to listen to you two squabbling.'

'Yep, go git your rope, Wilf. Tie up these two *hombres*. And the fat frump, too, if she don't stop her caterwauling.' Clint picked up the surrendered firearms and tossed them in the stream. 'Come on, hand over any knives you're hiding. We ain't got all day. Snap to it.'

'Yeah, you're beginning to try my patience.' Wilf returned and began to hogtie the two Mexicans, ankles to wrists behind them, tight nooses around their necks. 'Personally, I'd prefer to slit your throats.'

Clint found a poncho and cape in the coach which the two men had brought along, presumably in case of rain. He picked up their sombreros. 'These should come in handy. Shove our *amigos* in the shade, Wilf. We don't want to fry their brains.'

'Jeez! What are you, some goody-goody? You sure you got the guts to shoot a man, mister, 'cause we may well have to!'

'I only shoot to kill if it's necessary,' the ranger replied. 'Maybe that's where you and I differ.' He brandished the Peacemaker at the two females. 'Come on, get back in the coach. Just keep your mouths shut and do as we tell you. Let's hit the trail, Wilf.'

NINE

Clint Anderson hauled the low-slung landau off the trail out of sight amid the branches of the willow grove. He swung around on the box and slid down into the front seat beside Teresa. 'We need some information. Where would Three Fingers Jack be right now?'

'Eef I help you' – the girl's eyes, as sultry as sloes, were smouldering with either anger or daring, he wasn't sure which – 'you take me to America del Norte?'

'I dunno.' He didn't want to make promises he couldn't keep. 'Maybe.'

'Sure he will.' Wilf Stringer was sitting opposite, one arm around the shoulders of the portly Maria. He reached forward his other hand and patted Teresa's knee. 'You can count on that, baby. We'll take you both to the land of the free.'

Teresa looked doubtful, but she slid her arm into Clint's hugging him to her. 'The sun is at its highest.

At two Jack will take a siesta. He will expect me home to lie with him in the sheets. Ugh! I hate that man.'

'What about the *vaqueros*?'

'*Sí*, they take a rest, too. It is the custom in Mexico. They start work again about four.'

'That means we've got an hour or so to kill,' Clint told Stringer. 'We want to get there when they're getting dozy and off guard.'

'Great. Time for a bit of relaxation 'fore we go into battle.' Wilf grinned gappy teeth and gave the *duenna* a squeeze. 'She ain't a bad-looking old broiler, this one.'

Maria was, indeed, well-fleshed beneath her black silk dress, her luxuriant hair streaked with silver, her nose protruberantly aristocratic, dark eyes staring mournfully. She tried to struggle away, calling out in Spanish, 'Leave me alone! Who are you? What do you want with Señor Artemio?'

'Señor Artemio?' Wilf pronounced the words with sarcasm. 'We've come to confiscate anything valuable he's got. He's a bad man and his cash ain't his. But right now I've taken a fancy to you. How about it, darlin'?'

'Quit it, Stringer. She's been through enough already. She don't need the extra shock of a fat oaf like you hammering at her. I ain't a man who countenances rape.'

'Who said anything about rape?' Wilf took a roll of greenbacks from his pocket and peeled off four five-dollar bills. He waved them under the woman's nose like he would a carrot to tempt a donkey. 'Howja like to earn twenty dollars. That's half-a-year's salary to you, ain't it? This stuff works miracles, don't it?'

Maria's eyes bulged with greed, but she crossed herself and, looking guiltily at Teresa, cried, 'May the Lord forgive me.'

The girl shrugged. 'Don't hesitate on my account.'

Stringer produced another ten dollars and tucked them into her bosom. 'The Lord ain't gonna give you thirty dollars, is he? Come on, let's take a stroll down by the river-bank.' He pushed her gently out of the coach, stepped out after her and gave them a wink. 'Doncha worry. Take it easy. We're all gonna be rich in an hour or two.'

Clint sighed as the lovebirds wandered off. 'At least it's stopped her squawking. Nothing worse than a screaming woman.'

The girl peered at him and gave a little smile. 'What you gonna do with Señor Jack?'

'Take him, and his stolen loot, back to the States with any luck.'

'Why you not keel him?' Teresa spat the words out in broken English. 'He ees bad man. He get drunk, tie me up naked, beat me, make me do bad theengs.'

'How old are you?'

'Seventeen and half.' Teresa reached up to untie the scarlet ribbon tying back her dark hair and shook it out to flow about her heart-shaped face. 'I not a keed. I a woman now.' She put a hand on his thigh and snuggled closer. 'Promise me you take me to

America. I be good to you. I know how to make man happy.'

'Yeah, I bet you do. But it ain't as easy as that.'

'Why it not easy?' Teresa's peach-coloured complexion glowed with indignation. 'You easy take me to America.'

He couldn't help laughing. 'What would I do with you there?'

'You marry me. I make a good wife for you.'

'Yeah?' There was a merriment and a sadness dancing in the dark pools of her eyes as they met his. A strange sensation hit him that they were looking into each other's souls. 'How about if I tell you I'm here for that necklace, the gold one with rubies.'

'The necklace? But that is mine. Jack gave it to me.' Her face quivered, despondently. 'It is all he has given me.'

'It was not his to give. It's stolen property. I'm a peace officer from Texas. I'm here to get it back.'

'A lawman?'

'Yep. Texas Ranger. Aw, come on.' He took her small hand in his and gave it a squeeze. 'I'll buy you another necklace. One that ain't stole.'

'You think I am Jack's whore? That's what they all say. Once a whore always a whore.' She spoke in Castilian with a bitterness to her tone. 'You think all I want from you is to take me away from this prison, to take me to America. You think I lie to you.'

'If you've only been with one man and you were forced to go with him you ain't a whore. That's my

113

opinion. You're just a gal who's had a rough deal. But there's no easy answers. I got things to do. I may likely be lying dead 'fore this night's out.'

'No, don' say that.' She reached up a hand to tenderly stroke his cheek. 'Don' leave me. It's not just I wanna go America. It ees that you – you are the first man I meet I wan' be with. I mean, for always.'

'Look, I like you, too.' He kneaded the back of her slim neck, absentmindedly. 'But I got problems. I gotta work out how to get Jack.'

'I tell you the layout of house. I help you. You take the necklace. I don' care. That is nice what you do to me. Jack is never gentle with me like this.'

'It ain't just Jack.'

'Whass the matter? You got a wife?'

'Not a wife. Another woman. Call me old-fashioned, but I believe in being faithful to one gal.'

' 'Course you do. You nice man. But she ees long way away,' the girl murmured, and her delicate fingers began to explore the thigh in his jeans above the leather chaps, probing upwards, creeping like spider's legs up around his crotch. 'Perhaps you forget her this afternoon.'

'She's a married woman.'

'Married? Huh! In that case you forget her for good.' Her fingers expertly unpopped the studs of his flies and slid inside. 'You like that?' She smiled sweetly up at him. 'You wan' me be good girl? Or you wan' me to be whore? I can be both.'

'Aw, hail,' he groaned, for he was a man like any

114

other. 'You just do what you feel like doing, honey.'

An hour must have passed before he returned to his senses. He rested with her in his arms, and watched the butterflies fluttering, preparing for their journey north. 'Well, whadda ya know?' he said. 'You certainly are a beaut. I might take you back to America with me, after all. What's your name, by the way?'

'Teresa.' She smiled and kissed him. 'I am named after saint. Do you know what I thank God for? That I have not had Jack Artemio's child.'

'I would second that. My name's Clint.' He offered his hand. 'Pleased to meetcha.'

He could hear Stringer noisily bragging and fooling about along the creek. 'Hey, fatso,' he shouted, standing up in the coach and buckling on his gunbelt. 'Leave that woman alone and git your butt up here. It's time we went to work.'

'I'm a man of strongly amorous propensities.' Stringer affected a scholarly air as he emerged from the bushes. 'I can no more alter my nature than could a fox change his ways and give up raiding henhouses. What you two been up to?'

'Oh, nothing much. Discussing the works of Plato. Here!' Anderson tossed him a sombrero and a poncho. 'Put these on.'

Stringer did so, adjusting the gaudy striped *serape* over his shoulders and belly and Manolo's tall, pointy-crowned wide-brimmed hat on his head. 'How do I look?'

'Friggin' ridiculous.' Clint draped Jorge's cape over his shoulders and tried on his sombrero. 'How about me?'

Teresa giggled. 'Not as stupid as that fat peeg.'

'Thank you.' Wilf grinned, as he broke open his shotgun to check its load and snapped it shut again, cocking the dual hammers. 'I've always been admired for my sartorial air.'

Clint levered the first of twelve slugs out of the magazine into the breech of his Winchester carbine and put it under his boot as he gathered the reins of the greys. 'If you two ladies would like to take your seats. Remember, if any shooting starts duck down and stay put. Us two will abandon ship so you won't be a target.'

The two females had refreshed themselves at the stream and looked as innocent as daisies as they sat back in the coach. The two Americans knew they were going into something they might not come out of alive, but after the activities of the afternoon all four were somehow gay and cheerfully relaxed.

'Giddap.' Clint set the greys moving out of the trees. 'You ready for this picnic, Wilf?'

'Sure am.' Stringer patted the stock of the shotgun. 'Let's go, *amigo.*'

Jack Davis was sprawled in a shiny cowhide and horn armchair in the banqueting hall of the spacious hacienda where once Spanish conquistadors would have caroused.

'Where's that li'l bitch got to?' he wondered, consulting his gold watch. 'Time she was back.'

It never occurred to Jack that young Teresa might find another lover. She wouldn't dare. She knew the consequences. He had her well watched when she went into town, but maybe he would have to stop these trips up-river. 'I don't trust no one,' he said, stroking the head of a big hound that gazed at him lovingly. 'You're my only pal.'

He spun the cylinder of the Dragoon revolver, which he stuck into his holster as he got to his feet. He pulled a hat down over his thick hair to shade his surly features and prowled out into the courtyard. Where the hell was she? Why was she late?

'Coach coming!' one of the lookouts stationed above the main gates sang out. 'It is Señorita Teresa.'

'Good,' Jack growled. 'About time. Open the gates.'

Clint could see two men standing at their posts above the gates, rifles in their hands, but they did not look unfriendly. The gates were being opened and, as they drew near one of them shouted, 'Hey, Jorge, where you been? The *jefe* will roast your hide.'

'I'm a strong believer in getting my shot in first,' Stringer muttered, raising the twelve gauge and blasting the sentry who had spoken off his perch. He swung the weapon and, before the second lookout could react, gave him the same treatment with the second barrel. 'Bull's-eye!'

'Hyaahhrgh!' The ranger sent the greys charging forward through the gates and hauled in outside the front door of the house. He grabbed his Winchester as a bullet whanged past his head splintering the coach's footboard. He leaped down and rolled behind a stone horse trough for cover. Peering upwards he located the guard in the tower as more bullets scorched too close for comfort. He took careful aim and squeezed out three shots in quick succession. 'Got him,' he gritted out as the lookout tumbled, somersaulting from the tower.

'What the hell's going on on?' Jack Davis stood on the front steps of his house, his heart pounding, frozen with fear and panic. 'Who are they?' he wondered. Several *vaqueros* were running from the bunkhouse. 'Get them!' he screamed and backed into the house, slamming the oak door shut and bolting it. He stood listening to the sound of battle then ran upstairs, cocking the Dragoon. Maybe he could get them from the window.

Wilf Stringer had jumped from the coach and, as the *vaqueros* began shooting leaped over the stout wooden stockade of the corral to escape their lead. He pulled out his trusty Colt Frontier and peered over the top of the corral rail, picking his targets, although he couldn't see much through the dust kicked up by the frightened coach horses and the drifting gunsmoke. But he gave two more Mexicans a taste of his lead.

Wilf was blithely unaware he had landed in a pen

of wild bulls until he heard a snorting sound, and turned to see one pawing the sand, head down, his eyes blazing with anger, his knife-sharp horns aimed at him. Stringer tried to get away but he was too fat and ungainly to evade the charge. He was hit full on by a ton of hide and prime beef muscle, the horns ripping into his guts, the head tossing him into the air like a rag doll. He gasped as he hit the sand, but the beast wasn't going to give up, maddened and swinging at him. Wilf screamed as the horns got him in the groin.

Wilf managed to struggle to his knees as the bull backed off and, his face aghast, he saw a *cibilero* riding alongside the rail, a lance raised in his fist. He hurled it, not at the bull, but at Wilf. It thudded into his chest and sent him sprawling back into the dust. 'Aw,' Wilf moaned, 'just my luck!'

Clint Anderson was still pinned down behind the horse trough although his accurate shooting with the Winchester had made the *vaqueros* back off. But he was down to his last slug. In a lull in the shooting he reached for the dynamite in the warbag slung over his shoulders, found his strikes, lit a fuse and hurled the stick at the front door.

Ker-rumpf! The oak door crashed backwards, taking a good bit of the masonry with it.

Anderson abandoned the carbine and, Peacemaker at the ready, charged forward and leaped through firing blindly at whoever might be there. A bullet ripping through his shirt sleeve made him dive sliding for cover beneath the banqueting table and alerted him to an assailant at the top of the stairs.

Jack Davis peered through the banister rail and loosed a fusillade of shots from the Dragoon in his hands down at the ranger, but the oak refectory table was too tough to penetrate, the bullets bouncing off like rubber.

Pinned down, Clint returned fire as best he could and waited for a lull in the proceedings. At that moment Teresa stepped through the rubble around the doorway, his Winchester carbine held across her chest.

Jack's Dragoon was empty and he roared down at her, 'Bring that up to me.'

'Don't do it, Teresa,' Clint shouted. 'Stay back.'

The girl glanced at him and nimbly climbed the staircase to the landing. Jack tossed the revolver clattering away and held out a hand to her. 'Good gal, give it me.'

'Certainly,' she smiled. 'I'll give it you. Where do you want it?' She had turned the business end of the carbine on him from three paces away. 'In the gut? Or between the eyes?'

'You wouldn't dare,' he growled, extending his hand. 'Don't play games. Just give it me.'

'It's me who's in charge now, Jack. How do you like that?' Teresa's dark eyes held his malevolent regard and her finger took first pressure of the trigger. 'You want it, do you?'

Davis licked his lips, unsure whether she had the nerve to fire. He took a step towards her and as he did so Teresa swung the carbine down, pressing it against his boot. Jack tried to grapple with her. An explosion crashed out. There was a shout of pain. As the ranger arrived at the top of the stairs Davis was hopping about, cursing luridly. 'That bitch. She's shot me.'

'That's what you asked for, didn't you?' she replied.

Clint caught hold of Three Fingers Jack and frisked him, taking his knife, kicking his gun away. 'OK, you're under arrest. I'm a ranger. I'm taking you back to Texas.'

There were excitable shouts from down below as three *vaqueros* climbed through the rubble, guns in their fists. Anderson hauled Davis in front of him by the scruff of his collar and yelled, 'I'm a United States law officer. This man is a wanted criminal and I'm taking him to Texas for trial. Don't try anything, or he'll get my first bullet through the brain. Either way you look at it none of you will be working for him any longer. So, back off out of the house.'

Davis retched with pain and groaned, 'For Christ's sake do something about my foot. Clear off, boys, don't make him do it.'

His fierce foreman, Raoul, was hesitant, but finally shrugged and beckoned the others to retreat.

'Wise-thinking. Teresa, get his key. Let's take a look in that safe.'

'She don't know where the key is,' Jack snarled.

'Yes, I do, I watched you hiding it one night when you thought I was asleep.' The girl led the way down the staircase to the study, Davis hopping after her, prodded by Clint's Peacemaker. She found the keys tucked behind a loose stone in the chimney piece and brandished them, smiling triumphantly, finding the key to fit the big safe. 'Ta-ra!' she cried, as the door swung open. 'Behold the miser's wealth.'

Even Anderson was momentarily dumbfounded by the leather bags full of gold coins, each holding $500. 'Whoo!' He made a quick estimation. 'There must be twenty thousand dollars.'

'Twenty-five,' Davis corrected, with a groan. 'Teresa, get my boot off, will ya? Let's take a look at what you've done to me.'

'I'm not your lackey any more, Señor Jack,' she said. 'Haven't you got that in your thick skull yet?'

'Three thousand of that cash is legitimately mine,' Davis muttered. 'From the sale of my bulls. Why don't you take the rest and go? Let me stay here with my ranch. I ain't gonna hurt nobody no more. What's the good of taking me back?'

'You touch my emotions, mister, and I'm inclined to agree,' the ranger murmured, as he examined a bag of coins. 'But the law's the law and I'm sworn to uphold it. I'm a man of my word and I've gotta take you back. Don't worry, they won't hang you. You'll probably just get ten years hard labour on the chain gang.'

'You'll never get me outa Mexico. The *rurales* will

see to that. I'm a friend of the governor, ain't I, Teresa?' Davis cursed them again. 'I'm not going back to the pen.'

'If this is your cash,' Clint remarked, clinking $500 in gold in one sack, 'why don't we go give it them outside as a sort of bonus?'

'I'll give it them,' Teresa cried, taking it from him. 'I'll give them the key to his wine cellar, too. They can all get drunk.'

'Good, that should keep 'em quiet, or friendly, should I say. Where's Wilf got to?'

Teresa stopped in her tracks. 'He's dead. Didn't you know? A bull gored him.'

'Shee-it. Are you sure?'

'Sure I'm sure.'

'That damn fool. What a way to go.' Anderson shook his head, sadly. 'I liked that guy. But I guess he knew the odds.'

Outside the front door a bunch of the remaining *cibeleros* and *vaqueros*, some bloodily battle-scarred, *peons*, grooms and serving wenches, were gathered in noisy debate.

'Hey, it's fiesta time. Jack and I are leaving you.' Teresa took handfuls of gold coins and tossed them around as if she were feeding the hens. Men, women, girls squealed and laughed and dived to recover what they could. 'And here's the key to the cellar.' She offered it to Raoul. 'Go roll out a cask. Enjoy life while you can before the *rurales* come.'

Teresa was enjoying distributing Jack's largesse.

She went and unhitched Rocky and Wilf's horse from the back of the landau and led them through the rubble into the house. 'Here we are,' she called, with girlish enthusiasm. 'We can start loading up.'

'Yep. You stick what you can in their saddle-bags, I'll take the rest out to that coach. There's quite a cache of gold to carry.' He grinned at her. 'That was a crazy thing to do, Teresa, but brave of you.'

Her eyes shone lustrously as she returned his smile. 'Manolo showed me how to handle the coach. I will drive it for you to America. You can sit in the back with Jack.'

'You're a crafty l'il minx, aincha? You've got it all worked out.' He grinned at her again. 'But I guess I'll have to keep an eye on Jack if I'm gonna get him out.'

'Do we have to take him?'

He stroked his jaw with a worried look. 'Let's say I've gotta try. I'm a ranger. And, anyway, there's five thousand dollars bounty on his head.'

It took a while to get loaded and by that time Jack's former employees were reeling about, singing, shouting, playing guitars, bottles of fine wine and brandy in their hands, having a fine old time, for who knew what the morrow would bring. Living might be cheap in Mexico, but life was even cheaper.

'*Andale*!' Teresa had attired herself in *vaquero*'s costume, a stiff-brimmed hat set jauntily. She sat on the box holding the reins as Clint helped shove the blood-booted Jack inside the landau. 'Let's go,' she shouted, cracking her whip and setting the greys off at a spirited trot through the open gates. 'Goodbye, Maria. *Adios, muchachos.*'

Clint took a last look back at Wilf, sprawled gorily, sighed, and said to Davis, 'Maybe I oughta put the hood up? It looks like rain.'

Three Fingers Jack didn't reply. He merely groaned, a sick look on his face.

ELEVEN

'So now we can call you Three Toes Jack!' Teresa giggled as she cut away Davis's boot to reveal his smashed foot. The big toe and the one next to it had been blown off by the close impact of the bullet.

'Very funny,' he gasped. 'I'll get even with you, you two-timing whore. I ain't finished yet.'

'Do you want me to help you or not?'

'Yeah, yeah,' he urged, 'go on.'

She bathed his foot in a bowl of hot water, tried to staunch the blood with plugs of rag and bandaged it as best she could. 'We got to keep you alive to get the reward on you. That's why I do this.'

They had reached Rosita mid-evening and were bedding down in the stable at her family's adobe shack.

Clint deemed it best to rest the horses before they went on.

'We go have supper with them,' Teresa said. 'Can I give them some gold? I may not ever see them again.'

'Sure, why not. I'll deduct it as expenses.' The ranger grinned and passed her a sack of $500. 'Tell them it's from the grateful Señor Artemio for their hospitality.'

Davis scowled at him. 'You'll be laughing on the other side of your face soon. You'll never get through Zaragoza. I got friends there.'

'We'll see.' The ranger knew there could be trouble and decided to hang around awhile the next morning. It might be best to go through the main town at night-time. Teresa walked into the village but nobody seemed aware anything was amiss. There was no sign of pursuit.

'They'll still be getting drunk on Jack's wine. He has many casks in the cellar!' she said.

There was an ominous rumble of thunder as their carriage rattled through the narrow cobbled streets of Zaragoza. Darkness had fallen by the time they reached the town and the townspeople paid them little heed. Most were indoors at dinner and an appetizing scent of spiced cooking drifted from the barred windows of the ancient houses. A sudden flash of lightning illuminated three corpses hanging from the bough of a manzanita tree in the main square. On a piece of cardboard pinned to one was scrawled, '*Criminales.*'

Teresa drew the landau in outside a cantina, turned to them and sang out, 'I'm hungry. Are we going to eat?'

Clint frowned. 'It ain't a good idea to stop. I want to get through this town as fast as possible.'

'What's the matter?' Three Fingers Jack asked. 'You getting jittery? You worried they might string you up, too?'

'You better not say a word outa tune,' Clint gritted out, digging his Peacemaker into Davis's side, 'or it'll be the last thing you do.'

But he was feeling peckish himself, so he handed her some coins. 'First water the horses, then go in and buy something we can chew on as we go along. Don't delay; I've gotta keep an eye on this monkey.'

The two horses hitched to the back snickered when they smelt water and Teresa led them around to the trough where the coach pair were drinking. With her hair tied up under her hat, wearing tight, flared pants and embroidered velvet jacket, and her riding boots, she would pass for a slim youth in the shadow, but in lamplight her face had a girl's delicacy of structure.

The square was deserted but for a few beggars and fruit vendors. The ranger felt tense and uneasy as he waited in the coach. The horses could do with another rest but they would have to go on.

Jack Davis eyed the corpses and growled, 'The Grim Reaper's no stranger in these parts. You're never gonna make it, ranger. You might as well let me go. I'll keep my mouth shut.'

'Shut up. I'd rather trust a rattlesnake.' Clint was relieved to see the girl emerge from the cantina with a paper bag of goodies in her arm. But then his heart sank as a sharp-faced *mestizo* in a green uniform, the peaked cap and scarlet band of lieutenant of *rurales*, stepped out, watching her. Worst of all, he quickly followed her to the coach, helped her climb onto the box.

'*Buenas tardes*, Señor Artemio.' He clicked his heels and saluted. 'Late to be out driving, isn't it?'

'Yeah, I was just thinking of stretching my legs.' Jack started to get up. 'I'll jine ya for a drink.'

'No.' Clint nudged him with the revolver in his back as Davis began to haul himself up. 'We ain't got time.'

'I thought I recognized Teresa.' The flickering oil lamp hung outside the cantina cast a wan look over the lieutenant's yellow-hued features which had a Mongolian cast. Probably his Indian mother had mated with a Chinese settler on the coast. 'Is she learning to drive? Where is your coachman, *señor*?'

'You may well ask,' Jack replied. 'That's what I'd like to know.'

A bunch of *rurales* in sombreros, strung with bandoliers of bullets, their blood-red capes slung back over their shoulders, was spilling out of the cantina. An ugly-looking lot, they were toting carbines and were curious to see what was going on.

The lieutenant peered through his upslanted eyes at the ranger. 'I haven't met this *Americano* before. He seems eager to be on his way. No, I insist, you must all step out and join us.'

129

'No way,' Clint shouted. 'We're in a hurry. Go on, Teresa, give 'em the whip.'

But, shielded by the side of the coach the lieutenant had undone his holster and drew it to cover Anderson. 'Stop!' he commanded. 'That's an order.'

Suddenly he realized that the ranger had a revolver in his fist and without hesitation fired. Clint ducked back as the bullet grazed his temple. He extended his arm point blank and blasted the Mexican between the eyes.

Teresa lashed at the greys, setting them off at a fast trot as the lieutenant fell back in a pool of blood.

All hell broke loose among the *rurales*, who ran towards them firing wildly with carbines and revolvers. Just at that moment Jack Davis decided to make a break; swinging open the coach door, standing up on his good foot, he tried to leap to safety. In the split second that he stood poised a slug from one of the *rurales* hit him in the chest. He gasped with pain and shock and toppled back into the coach.

'Hee-yagh!' Teresa shrilled, whipping at the horses and sending the coach careering around the plaza on two wheels. Clint hung on, thinking they were surely turning over. But they bounced back onto four again as the *rurales* sent a fusillade of lead carooming after the fugitives.

'Hagh!' Teresa shouted again, straightening up and sending the carriage at breakneck speed charging through the town gate and out onto a winding trail.

'Hell's bells!' Clint moaned, as he hung on. Jack Davis was laid across him, blood pouring from his chest, dead as the proverbial dodo. He shoved him onto the front seat and picked up his Winchester. 'Now we're in real trouble.'

Railroads were as yet unknown in Mexico, although the Southern California company had plans to push south from Tucson. Telegraph wires, too, had yet to be strung across the wild, mountainous country. The Spanish had done little road building except where they needed to haul their booty of gold to the coastal ports. Travel was confined to coach, horseback, mule, *burro* or shanks's pony along trails often blocked by floods or landfalls. So remote were some villages that they had yet to hear that Porfirio Diaz was their new president. All military dispatches had to be sent by fast horse courier.

Captain Anderson reflected that this might well aid their escape back to the border, even though at that very moment he was being bounced so severely in the back of the carriage as Teresa careered the greys at a gallop along the tortuous trail he could barely take aim with his Winchester at a troop of *rurales* who were on their tail.

A vehicle like theirs, and a pair of horses who had already covered fifty miles in two days, was no match for the high-spirited mustangs of the *rurales* who, he could see in the ghostly moonlight, were fast gaining on them. On top of which there was the ever present danger any moment of the landau losing a wheel and somersaulting them all over a yawning precipice at the side of the trail to be smashed to pieces on the rocks below.

They were weaving down the mountainside from a height of 2,000 feet, Teresa, if anything, whipping the horses faster with the aid of the gradient.

'Slow down,' the Texan yelled. 'You'll kill us all.'

'I wanna get to the bridge,' Teresa screamed, not looking back, 'before *they* do.'

'What bridge?' Then he remembered the iron suspension bridge built over a deep ravine by the French when, for a short while, they were masters of Mexico. The landau was bouncing and swaying so much, the horses at both front and back careering along, wild-eyed, in the moonlight that it was fruitless trying to get a shot at their pursuers. He laid the Winchester aside and, digging in his heels to steady himself, took a stick of dynamite from his warbag. But at this speed it was impossible to light the fuse. 'For Christ's sake, slow down,' he shouted. 'Now! Before we get near the bridge.'

It was approached by a narrow high-walled lane blasted through the mountainside. The girl hauled back on the reins and managed to slow the horses, who were too exhausted to wish to do much else. 'Good,' Clint muttered as he struck a match and lit the dynamite fuse. The charging, pistol-packing *rurales* were closing fast and now only seventy yards behind.

'Come on,' Clint hissed, brandishing the fuse to

make it burn faster. 'Here's something you ain't expecting.'

As the *rurales* galloped into the ravine he hurled the dynamite back overboard. There was a mighty explosion as it detonated, blowing up a hail of dust and rocks. The ranger peered back through the drifting cloud and saw a pile of rubble was blocking the pass. It had brought the *rurales* to a halt.

He stood forward and laid a hand on Teresa's shoulder as she calmed their startled horses. 'Take it easy over the bridge. We don't wanna git stuck.'

It was a solid construction with iron supports on both sides, rivets as big as a man's fist. The French engineers had made a good job of it. Steel wires suspended a flooring of wooden struts which rattled as they drove across. The struts were solid enough. It was the landau that had taken too much of a beating. There was an ominous crack as they reached the far side and the coach lurched lopsided on a broken axle, half-over the gulch. 'Holy tarnation!' Clint gave a whistle as he peered down through a giddy expanse of air to a silver rivulet rushing along 500 feet below.

'I ain't going without the gold,' he said. 'Bring Rocky and Wilf's bronc forward. Unharness the greys and start loading the gold onto them out of the coach. I brought some big panniers along just in case we needed 'em. Lucky I did.'

'What are *you* going to do?' she asked.

He produced the last four sticks of dynamite from his warbag. 'You'll see.' He hurried back across the bridge then started to string the dynamite at intervals to the struts. He glanced back along the ravine as he worked. Several *rurales* were climbing over the hill of rubble and running towards him. He took a deep breath and forced himself to concentrate, lighting each fuse and hurrying back to the coach. He grabbed his Winchester and knelt to take aim.

'Are you ready, Teresa? Lead them horses away from here. I'll stay and give 'em something to think about.'

The girl had managed to load the horses and struggled to haul the four of them along the trail. 'Come on, boys,' she urged.

Clint levered the Winchester and triggered out shots that whined past the *rurales*, making them dive for cover. A more foolhardy *rurale* came on. Clint fired again and saw him topple, clutching his torn leg. The fuses were fizzling and flaring. 'Time to go,' he said. He stood and waved his carbine at the Mexicans. 'So long, *amigos*.'

He ran to join Teresa and turned to see the bridge go up in smoke, girders, bolts and wire hurled into the air, the whole edifice disintegrating as if in slow motion. The carriage slid to one side and went spinning, also, down into the gulch. Some of the *rurales* ran up in the moonlight to peer over the edge.

'They won't come after us tonight. We can take it easy,' he said to the girl. 'We'll lead the horses on foot. It'll give 'em a breather. They are our passport out.'

'Are you hurt? 'she asked. 'What's that blood dripping from you?'

'It's not me, it's Jack.' He grinned and produced a severed hand that he had chopped from the corpse with his Bowie. 'I've gotta prove he's dead, ain't I, if I'm gonna collect?'

TWELVE

The skies darkened and the rain sheeted down as they plodded their horses back along the trail towards the border. Clint, a week's stubble on his jaw, in sombrero and water-streaming slicker, looked more like a desperado than a ranger, and Teresa, in muddy boots and Manolo's cape, not much different. When, mid-morning they reached a cluster of adobe houses, set amid patches of maize, he called out, 'Let's take a break.'

It was a flyblown hole, naked children splashing in brown puddles in the rutted street, curs yapping at the horses' hoofs, women in black *rebozos* peering from doors to watch them pass by. But there was a cantina, a scrawled notice in Spanish advertising, 'Rooms – Typhoid Free Showers.' He guessed it attracted occasional passing trade.

A bunch of locals in their ragged cotton pyjamas were sheltering from the downpour. They fell silent as Clint and Teresa entered, assessing them with sullen eyes. 'Howdy,' he muttered, and ordered coffee at a makeshift bar.

'How much further to the border?' Teresa asked.

'Not far now.' After the journey from Rosita and flight from Zaragoza they had been walking and riding in turns, bypassing Piedras Negras and pushing on through the dawn. 'I dunno about you but I'm just about dead on my feet. Could do with a couple of hours' shut-eye 'fore we cross the Rio Grande and head through Eagle Pass.'

'Is it safe?' she asked. 'What about the *rurales*?'

'Aw, I think we've left them behind. Without their loo-tenant they'd be like headless chickens, running around waiting for new orders.'

They paid a few pesos for a room and feed for their horses, put them around the back and lugged the gold-crammed saddle-bags and panniers inside. There was a musty store in the village and the ranger went across and bought a bottle of vinegar and a glass jar. 'What you want that for?' she asked.

'Pickle Jack's hand. Darn flies are buzzing all around my bag. Just as well I didn't bring his head, too.'

'God rest his evil soul.' Teresa crossed herself and giggled. 'I theenk I take a typhoid-free shower and dry out my wet clothes.'

'Yep. I think I'll jine ya.'

The 'shower' was in a corner of the wash-house behind their room. It consisted of a bucket in a contraption of ropes. They stood beneath and he tugged at a string which tipped the 'typhoid-free' water into another bucket riddled with holes. It would have been fine if the string hadn't snapped. 'Ouch!' The bucket caught him a painful blow on the head as it clattered down. 'That's all I need,' he groaned.

He found Teresa lying naked on the filthy stained mattress of an iron bed. 'Let's hope it's bug free,' he muttered, as he dried himself. But when he lay down with her she smelt soap-sweet and enticing and, if there were any fleas a-roaming, he forgot all about them as he took her in his arms. The girl hung onto him, her slim arms tight around his neck as the bed rattled rhythmically against the wall. 'I never want to let you go,' she cried, in a kind of ecstatic agony. 'You won't leave me, will you?'

'No, sure I won't, honey,' he murmured.

What more could he say? But what about Kathleen? As he lay back on the mattress a while later he remembered Wilf Stringer's words. Could there be a grain of truth in them? Was her professed love for him the real thing? Or would she, as Stringer claimed, in a couple of years betray him?

As if reading his thoughts, Teresa asked, 'What about your other woman?'

'It was jest one of them things. A lightning bolt that knocks you out for a while. She's a lady of the salon. It'd never work out 'tween us on a ranch. Whereas you, this last day or two I've seen you in action, you've got what it takes.' He idly stroked her

138

dark ringlets, then raised himself to kiss her. 'To tell you the truth, Teresa, you're the first gal I've met since my wife was killed that I feel easy with.'

He didn't remember falling asleep such was his exhaustion, a deep sleep of several hours from which he was rudely awoken. The cold steel of the barrel of a Colt Frontier was being pressed against his forehead. Clint opened his eyes and met those of Major J.B. Johnson. They were cold blue, in bloodshot yellow, and unflinching.

'Waal, just look at lover boy. Caught with his pants down. Who's this l'il *señorita* you're seducin' now? Like you seduced and ruined my daughter.'

'I didn't ruin Mary,' Clint whispered, coming to terms with this sudden apparition. 'She came to me of her own accord. We loved each other. Can't you get that into your thick head?'

'Huh! How about Piper's fancy wife? She love you, too? What is this charm you got, lover boy? Don't think I don't know about you.'

'Who ees thees, Clint?' Teresa murmured, pulling the blanket up over her nakedness. 'What does he want?'

'I'll give you three guesses, little lady. What's in them saddle-bags, there, that's what I'm having,' the major replied, gruffly. 'Move over to t'other side of the bed. I wouldn't want his brains to splatter over you.'

'You wouldn't do that, J.B. You might have slaughtered Comanches, men, women and kids with impunity, even a few blacks and Mexicans, but you wouldn't kill one of your own.'

'Wouldn't I? Think again, Ranger. I'm gonna enjoy this.'

Teresa wriggled away and hissed, 'Who are you, meester? Why don' you leave us alone?'

'Meet Major J.B. Johnson, the loud-mouthed legend of the frontier,' Clint said. 'Think about this J.B., you've upheld the law for thirty years. You don't wanna cross the line now. You could never live with yourself. You ain't cut out to be some scumbag thievin' outlaw.'

'Don't you believe it,' the major growled, increasing pressure on the Frontier. 'I'm gittin' old. I need a grubstake. I've had a peek at how much you got while you was snoozin' with your whore. I'm taking the whole damn caboodle. You've done all the work for me. Mighty kind of you, Anderson. So long.' He cocked the Frontier and grinned broken teeth beneath his bushy white moustache. 'Or should I say good riddance.'

'Don't hurt the girl,' Clint gritted out. 'She don't know nuthin'.'

'She knows my name—'

'*Sí*, I do.' Teresa had wriggled aside, as instructed, and felt down under the bed, groping about. She came up with Anderson's Winchester carbine, jamming it into the major's side. 'I'm gonna write it on your grave.'

The major froze, his blue eyes bulging, agitatedly, beneath his bushy brows and hat brim. 'Put that away, girlie. You ain't got the nerve.'

'I'll think you'll find she has, J.B.,' Clint muttered. 'Looks like checkmate, don't it?'

'You—' Johnson cursed him, his face glowing red. 'OK. Let's make a deal. I want half of everything.'

Clint gave a flicker of a grin. 'Careful, J.B., you'll have an apoplexy. You know I can't do that. That gold ain't our property. We're rangers. We gotta take it back. We gotta abide by the law, J.B. It's the only way.'

The major whined, 'What have the rangers ever done for me? I need that cash, Captain.'

'No way,' Clint said. 'Teresa, there's a bullet in the spout of that thing. All you gotta do is squeeze the trigger.'

The major was weakening. 'OK. I'll take half of all rewards you get and half of the ten per cent on the cash returned. How much is there, by the way?'

'About twenty-four thousand, last count.' Clint raised his fingers and pushed the Frontier aside. 'It's a deal. You'll get, let's see, a couple of thousand. It's a fair slice and honest earned.'

'All right,' J.B. replied, grumpily. 'Tell her to take that gun outa my ribs. I'll help you take it back.'

Clint gave a sigh of relief as the guns were put aside. He reached for his pants. 'Glad you see sense, J.B. We'll just have a beer and a bite to eat and we'll be on our way.'

'Where's Three Fingers Jack?' the major asked. 'Did you get him?'

Clint nodded at the jar on the dresser. 'He's there.'

'What's on the menu?' the major demanded of the barman in his rough frontier Spanish.

The bald little Mexican shrugged and indicated a tray of fried grasshoppers alongside some chunks of frizzling pigskin on the stove with, needless to say, flies ever present at the feast.

'What happened to the damn pork, I wonder?' J.B. chomped on a chunk of fatty crackling. 'Why is everybody in this country so poverty-stricken?'

'Not everybody,' Clint corrected. 'Most. There's a few at the top who live in luxury.'

He chewed on a mouthful of grasshoppers himself, and peered into a cauldron of bean soup redolent of fiery chillis. 'Guess I'll risk a bellyful of this.'

The major raised a mug of coffee to his lips and spat it out. 'Ugh! They could get the best Jalapa berries and they serve this muck. It's water-weak and lukewarm.'

He jumped to his feet and went into a gloomy kitchen where he found a sink full of unwashed crocks, a fly-buzzing pile of rubbish and a sputtering fire presided over by an old hag with matted hair in a black dress that must have been stranger to a wash-tub for many a year.

'My coffee,' he shouted, brandishing the mug. 'I

want it hot. Not chilly. Not tepid. Hot as a volcano. You understand?'

The woman wiped snot from her nose on her sleeve and began to call on innumerable saints to testify that she had never before had a complaint from a customer.

'It's a wonder any have survived,' J.B. admonished her. 'Clean this place up. Throw on more charcoal. What you trying to do, poison us?'

While this scene was being enacted, a scurvy-looking bunch of five Mexicans, horsemen, not *peons*, in leathers and hung with iron, swaggered into the cantina and arranged themselves around the tin stove, drying out their rain-wet clothes. They were accompanied by a gringo, a mean-faced *hombre* in a tall Stetson, a heavy revolver slung on his hip.

They sat with their backs to Anderson and the girl, which he considered fortunate. 'Don't say anything, J.B.,' he hissed as the major returned. 'But there's somebody there we know.'

'Frank Jackson,' the major muttered, recognizing him from wayback, as one of the workshy louts who hung around Denton saloons causing mischief, a crony of Sam Bass before they both went to the bad. He was the main suspect as the man who escaped from Round Rock, too. 'There's bounty on him. So, he's riding with that bunch now, is he?'

Clint assessed the situation. 'There's six of them to two of us,' he muttered. 'Maybe we'd better leave Frank to another day and ride on.'

143

'I ain't leaving nobody. Where's your guts, man?'

'We've got enough to do, major. We don't need more trouble.'

'Rubbish.' J.B. looked up as the barman returned with his mug. 'Yes?'

'Coffee. Strong. Hot,' the barman said. '*Mucho caliente.*'

The major absentmindedly gulped a mouthful. 'Agh!' he cried as it burned his throat and he spat it out again.

One of the *viciosos* turned to look at him and laughed. He was a typical frontier thug, the kind Jackson *would* be in cahoots with. 'Wipe that leer off your ugly mug or I'll wipe it off for you.' Johnson got to his feet toting his Frontier. 'Jackson, you're under arrest.'

'Teresa,' Clint said, touching her hand. 'I want you to go outside and load the horses. Have them ready to ride.'

'No, I don' wan' to leave you.'

'Do as I say,' he insisted, and she carefully eased her way out past the sprawled bunch of *bandidos* who were swivelling around on their stools to give the major the once-over. Jackson was on the other side of the stove, his back to the wall. 'You talking to me?'

'Frank Jackson, a no-account bum from Denton. Remember me?' the major asked. 'I'm arresting you for the murder of Sheriff Morris Moore and Sheriff Grimes. Two good men I was personally acquainted with. We're taking you back to Round Rock to stand

144

trial. Are you coming quiet, or not?'

Jackson's face split into a nervous grin. 'What? Are you joking, mister? Get lost.'

'Who is this, Frank?'The big *hombre* who had laughed butted in. 'What he want?'

Clint slowly rose to his feet, his fingers touching the butt of his Peacemaker. 'We're Texas Rangers. This is between us and Frank. I would advise you men to keep out of this.'

'Yeah,' the major growled, 'in other words clear off, get outa here, now, pronto. *Vamos.*'

'You've got no jurisdiction this side of the border,' Jackson said in his buzz-saw nasal whine. 'You cain't arrest me. I know my rights.'

'What rights did you give Sheriff Moore and Sheriff Grimes before you gunned 'em down in cold blood?' the major said. 'Just unbuckle your gunbelt and let it slip to the ground. Come on, Jackson, I ain't got all day.'

The Mexicans had begun to get to their feet, preparing for action. There was no way they were going to back down. The big *hombre* snatched a gun from his waist sash. 'You go to hell,' he snarled.

The big man was the first to die as the major's Frontier barked and the slug sent him flailing back. One of his arms hit the L-shaped stove chimney pipe and it clattered apart showering smoke and dust into the room.

Clint fanned his Frontier, dodging back against the wall to avoid the lead roaring from the Mexicans' guns. As the smoke billowed he got on one knee and fired his last two slugs. Frank Jackson screamed as his revolver was sent spinning from his hand and the major finished him with a bullet in his guts.

It had all happened in a matter of minutes. As the black smoke lifted Clint saw that all their adversaries were lying sprawled in attitudes of death. Except one, a thin-faced man, trickling blood as he leaned back against the wall, but raising his six-gun to aim. 'Watch out, J.B.,' Clint shouted.

It was too late. Johnson was sent hurtling back onto the floor by the force of the bullet. 'Now you, meester,' the Mexican gasped. Clint raised his hands, waiting his chance to pounce. As he did so, Teresa appeared in the doorway, the Winchester gripped to her shoulder, and fired. The thin *bandido* tried, wildly, to defend himself, but Teresa's bullet riddled his forehead and he sat back in his chair, his eyes staring as if astonished.

'That the first man I keel,' she gasped out, turning the Winchester in a sweeping arc. 'I hope it the last, eh, *muchachos*?'

None of the *peons* were inclined to argue as Anderson knelt down to the major. The blood was draining from his countenance. He was sinking fast. Clint struck a match and lit the cigar that was still gripped in his teeth. Johnson sucked it alight. 'We did OK, didn't we?' he gasped, blood and smoke trickling from his lips. 'I told you we could take 'em.'

'Yeah, you did damn well, Major. I'll make sure the

whole of Texas knows you went down shooting.'

'I wouldn't have it any other way. Take care of yourself, Clint, you lucky son-of-a-gun. Take care of the li'l gal. Here,' he said, patting his cigar case. 'You can have the rest of these.'

'Thanks, J.B.,' Clint muttered, as Johnson's head slumped. 'You always did smoke a good cigar.'

'Best Cuban,' he muttered, hoarsely. 'Maybe I'm gonna go meet Mary. I'll tell her you're OK. I guess I—'

They were the last words he said as the life left him. Clint closed his eyelids and got to his feet as the barman wailed, 'Look at this mess, all these bodies. What am I going to do with them?'

There was $30 in greenbacks in J.B.'s cigar case. Clint tucked it in the man's apron pocket. 'Do me a favour, *amigo*, bury that man. Get him a headstone. That should cover the cost. Here, have this put on it' – he used the barkeep's pencil to scrawl on his pad – Major James B. Johnson, Texas Ranger, killed by outlaws, 1878. 'Can you do that?'

'*Sí, amigo*, I will do that, but this is too much.'

'Keep it, and you're welcome to anything you find on them others, too.'

They went outside and mounted up, leading the two greys and headed north at a hard lope. They swam the horses across the rain-swollen Rio Grande and, as they did so, streamers of sunlight broke forth from the dark clouds setting the sky ablaze.

'Doesn't that look like the golden portal of

heaven,' Teresa exclaimed. 'Sometimes I really believe—'

'Welcome to God's own country,' Clint said, pointing the horses towards Eagle Pass.

THIRTEEN

San Antonio's main square was crowded and noisy, thronged with market stallholders, as they rode their horses in and hitched them to the rail outside the town hotel.

'You keep an eye on the broncs and them valuable saddle-bags,' Clint told Teresa. 'I'm going in.'

There was a tinge of affronted fear in the girl's eyes. 'You go to see her, don't you? It is her you love, not me.'

'Calm down, Teresa. 'He hooked an arm around her waist and pulled her into him. 'You're my gal now, not her. I'm going to tell her so. I'm gonna return her jewellery and get the thousand dollars reward. Then I'll be back. I won't be long.'

'Well, you make sure she don' cheat you. I don' like the sound of that lady. An' don' you go geevin' her no reward, neither. You know what I mean?'

'Wimmin! Don't they go on.' He grinned and kissed her lips. 'This'll only take a few minutes then

149

we'll be on our way.'

When they had reached Crystal City he had sent a cable to Kathleen care of the post office in Houston.

NECKLACE SAFE STOP MEET ME AT SAN ANTONE STOP ELEVEN AM SEPT TWO STOP USUAL PLACE STOP MUST TALK STOP CLINT

She was waiting in the rundown room, sitting on the bed in a rustling yellow silk gown and he was struck, as before, by her sophisticated beauty, her shining blonde hair, her green gems of eyes staring at him out of wide whites. Clint swallowed his nervousness. This was going to be hard. He would rather step into a room full of rattlers than have to tell her they had to split.

'I saw you talking to your little Mex whore,' Kathleen said, icily. 'I credited you with better taste.'

She wasn't going to make it easy, getting catty before they had begun. He ignored the remark and she said, 'So, where is it?'

He had his carpet bag, with a couple of thousand dollars in gold and silver change, slung over his shoulder. He dumped it on the bed and reached inside to produce a dirty piece of rag in which the ruby necklace, earbobs and bracelet were wrapped. He laid them out on the bed. 'These were a gift to that young Mexican lady, but when I told her they were stolen property she agreed to return them. I reckon she deserves a thank you for that.'

Kathleen's eyes flashed haughtily as she picked up the necklace, weighed it in her palm and tipped it with the bracelet and earbobs into a silver-coloured reticule she was carrying. 'She wouldn't appreciate them,' she said. 'Did you know these gems are worth a fortune?'

'In that case, I don't want to sound ungentlemanly but maybe we should discuss the question of the reward your husband promised.'

'Reward? She sounded offended. 'Haven't I rewarded you enough? You've had your way with me.'

'Hang on, what you saying, that you were just trying to sweeten me?'

'Oh, Clint, I'm sorry. I've missed you so much.' Kathleen moved towards him, caught hold of him, putting her lips close to his to be kissed. 'It's just that it made me so mad when I saw you down there with that . . . that creature.'

He steeled himself to hold her away, angry now. 'She ain't a creature. Her name's Teresa. She's a very sweet gal. I gotta tell you the truth, Kathleen, I might well marry her. It was good between you an' me, but we both knew it weren't right. I think you must go back to your husband.'

'What?' She pulled herself back with scream of incredulity. 'You might *marry* her? *You* are leaving *me*? Who do you think you are?'

Hell hath no fury like a woman scorned, he knew, so he watched her warily as she fell back on the bed against the carpet bag and heard it clinking.

'What's all this?' she asked.

'Just some of the stolen cash in gold coin. I'm returning the whole damn lot to the governor to claim my ten-per-cent share.'

'So, that's why that little money-grubber's after you. I suppose she's down there hanging on to the rest of the loot.'

'We're all money-grubbers, ain't we? Me, you, we're no exception. Look, Kathleen, don't—'

'Good Lord! You've got a nerve. First you come to meet me and bring your little doxy. Then you boast of how much cash you've got and expect me to pay you for the return of my own property.'

'Forget the damn reward.' Clint picked up the bag and swung it over his shoulder. 'You're upset, Kathleen. I'd better go. There's no use arguing. It's over 'tween us.'

Kathleen went to the window and looked down into the street. 'You'd better think twice about that.'

Clint had reached the door, turned and asked, 'Why?'

'Because,' she said with a smile, 'my husband's outside. I think he's planning to kill you.'

George Piper's plan to pipe oil in Houston that summer had not paid off. The initial surveys had proved promising but every time they drilled they just ended up with a dry hole. The enterprise had eaten up cash, so he was closing down the Bay City

Oil Company and getting out.

He had arrived in San Antonio on the railroad and had unloaded the surrey, with its fringed suntop, he had brought along. He put his fast, high-trotting thoroughbred in the shafts and with a man beside him called Jake Fenton drove the surrey into the market place.

Jake was a hard-looking *hombre*, renowned as a fast shootist Piper used as a bodyguard and general help to do his dirty work. As a precaution he had, however, strapped on a gunbelt and revolver under the jacket of his summer suit.

'Come on, Jake,' he said, jumping down. 'Nobody's gonna blame me for killing the man who's got my wife in there.'

'No problem,' Jake muttered as he followed him into the hotel. 'I'll make mincemeat of him.'

'Which room are they in?' Piper demanded of the clerk as he stormed in. 'You know who I'm talking about.'

But he had no need to be told for Clint Anderson had stepped out of the room onto the landing and was now poised at the top of the narrow stairs staring down through the shadowy gloom.

'There's no need for this, Piper,' he called out. 'It's over. I'm leaving. She's all yours. Just let me pass and you won't see me again. Or, if you want to lay your guns aside we can slug it out round the back man to man if you want. I guess you're entitled.'

'You bet I'm entitled.' Piper had pulled back his

jacket to reveal the revolver, but he hesitated when he saw the ranger's long fingers touch the butt of his own sidearm. He swallowed his alarm and shouted up, 'You've been messing with my wife behind my back, you dirty bastard. You've got to pay.'

'Don't be stupid, Piper,' Clint gritted out.

Piper quickly stepped back behind the cover of the desk and hissed at Fenton, 'Get him, Jake.'

The ranger's Peacemaker came out like greased lightning as Jake pulled his six-gun. Both men fired. Black smoke billowed, but it was Jake who collapsed in a heap.

'Get outa here, Piper, you ain't got the guts for this,' Clint drawled, and carefully descended the stairs, smoking gun in hand.

Suddenly there was another clap of an explosion behind him and he crumpled as the bullet hit him in the back. He fell forward, tumbling down the stairs.

Kathleen stood at the top, a small two-shot derringer in her hands. Her eyes were blazing as she called, 'Is he dead, George?'

'Looks like it to me.' Piper nervously poked his boot into the apparently lifeless ranger sprawled across Jake Fenton, blood flowering in a patch on the back of his shirt. 'Have you got the necklace?'

'Yes.' Kathleen's face was grim, but somehow elated as she descended the stairs and pulled the carpet bag from Anderson's arm. 'Guess what's in this? Gold. And there's more on their horses outside.'

The desk clerk was frozen with horror, staring at the bodies on his floor. 'What,' he stuttered, 'is going on?'

Piper turned to him. 'Keep your mouth shut and you won't get hurt.'

Kathleen lowered her voice and whispered to Piper, 'He's got thousands in gold.' She took the ruby necklace from her reticule and handed it to him. 'Look at this. It's worked like a treat.'

'The dumb hick,' Piper said, pocketing it. 'How was he to know we stole it in the first place?'

'Not so fast!' Through the noise of the market-place Teresa had heard the muffled sound of gunshots. She paused only to get the Winchester from the saddle boot and ran into the rooming-house, appalled to see the ranger lying bleeding on the floor. She jabbed the carbine into Piper's side. 'Hold it right there!'

George Piper froze with fear and slowly raised his hands. 'Don't shoot,' he pleaded.

'You—' Teresa began to speak but there was the flash of an explosion from the small pistol concealed in Kathleen's hands. For a second Teresa stared into her vicious green eyes, then, as a terrible pain hit her, slid to the floor, leaving the wall streaked with blood. 'Oh, no,' she groaned.

'Serve her right, the stupid little whore,' Kathleen snapped, putting the derringer into her reticule. 'Come on, don't just stand there like an idiot, George. We must get away from here.'

'Somebody's been shot!' a stallholder shouted,

becoming aware above all the hubbub that there'd been a gunfight. A crowd gathered about him as they stood at the doorway of the hotel and peered inside. They paid little attention to a light surrey moving away down the street, a gentleman on the box driving, a lady in yellow sat beside him, two horses, heavily laden, loose-hitched at the back on leading ropes.

'It worked like a dream,' Kathleen said, 'The best scam we've ever pulled. We're rich, George.' She dug her hand into the bloodstained carpet bag to clutch for a handful of coins.

'Agh!' she screamed. Cold fingers seemed to be gripping her hand. She pulled back and saw a shrivelled, severed hand caught in her grip. 'Oh, my God,'she sobbed. 'What is it?'

George, too, looked startled. 'It's only got three fingers!'

'Get off!' Kathleen shook off the clinging hand and hurled it away onto the muddy street where a stray cur ran forward and began snarling and gulping at it.

'Come on,' she said, considerably shaken. 'Hurry!'

Piper flicked the whip across the thoroughbred and they went dashing away out of town.

Four weeks later Clint Anderson hauled in a buckboard outside the Fort Worth Cattlemen's Club. He climbed down, wincing with pain, for although a .22 didn't have much kicking power it could still inflict damage, or often kill. He was lucky that the slug had missed his vital organs by a fraction. The doc had dug out the small bullet but the wound had taken a long while to heal.

Teresa, arrayed today in a flowing, flame-coloured dress, which set off to perfection her slim, sun-dark body and mane of black curls, jumped down beside him, taking his hand as they climbed the steps to be greeted by Governor Dick Coke. He beckoned them into rattan armchairs on the veranda and asked, 'What's your poison, Captain?'

'I ain't captain any more. I've resigned,' Clint said, 'but a drop of what you're having wouldn't go amiss for medicinal purposes. Teresa might fancy a mint julep.'

The girl, too, had been brought back from the brink by careful nursing. The lead from the derringer had lodged in her ribs but had been extricated without too much loss of blood.

When the drinks were served Coke remarked, 'You've both made miraculous recoveries. Unfortunately, I've got bad news for you.'

'Shoot,' Clint said.

'The committee has refused to pay either of the rewards on Davis or Jackson. They say you've provided no proof that either of these men is dead. They've only got your word for it. Nor are they inclined to believe that you recovered any of the money. I'm sorry, Clint.'

'Yeah, so am I. Looks like I been wasting my time

don't it? I mighta known those jackals would renege on the deal.'

'No need to talk like that,' Coke said. 'I believe you, but the committee don't. Of course, if you were to go after Piper and get the money back, that's if he's really got it, as you say.'

'You know, I'm getting the feeling that they might suspect that I've buried the damn gold someplace and this is some cock 'n' bull story I've invented.'

'It does sound incredible,' Coke said. 'I mean, Piper was a highly respectable citizen.'

'Too respectable to try to murder us? So who did fire those guns?' Clint asked.

'Those two wicked ones,' Teresa butted in. 'They will find their own damnation.'

'Any news on him,' Clint asked, 'and his lady wife?'

'No.' The governor replenished their glasses. 'They've vanished leaving a lot of debts. It's very odd. The news is that they were seen boarding a schooner at Corpus Christi. It was bound for South America. But that's one hell of a big country. They could be anywhere.'

'Yep.' Clint Anderson rolled the whiskey around his mouth. It was an expensive brand. 'I guess they could.'

'You going after them?'

'Nope. I'll leave that to the Pinkerton men.'

'So.' The governor took a cheque from his pocket and passed it across. 'That's the five thousand reward on Sam, minus the two thousand paid to the widows and the other rangers like you instructed, and the thousand you promised to Murphy.'

Clint gave it a glance and drawled, 'I guess two thousand's better than nothing. Just as soon as I'm able to get back on a bronc we're heading for Wyoming. This should, at least set us up in stock. There's green grass and plenty of it up there, a chance for a man to make good. We'll be OK. Who needs all that cash?'

Coke offered his hand. 'No hard feelings I hope, Clint.'

'No, why should there be? I've found me this pretty gal and so happens we're about to get hitched.'

'*Sí.*' Teresa leaned forward with a smile and kissed him. 'And we're gonna have one long honeymoon.'

'Yeah,' Clint agreed, standing and taking her hand. 'You can count on that. How about you, Mr Coke? You fancy coming to the ceremony?'

'Why not?' The governor beamed and beckoned to the steward who opened the screen door to the billiards room. 'That goes for the rest of your gang.'

Laughing and hooting Lee Hall, Vern Wilson, Chris Connor and the rest of the Texas Rangers spilled out onto the veranda, milling around and congratulating Clint and Teresa.

'What's more,' Governor Coke yelled, hugging the girl, 'You'll have the wedding breakfast here, whiskey, champagne, all you boys can drink. It's all on me.'

AUTHOR'S NOTE

The theft of $60,000 from the Union Pacific express in 1877, equivalent to more than a million dollars today, was the second biggest train robbery of its era. Only $23,000 was ever recovered by the authorities. Jack Davis and Frank Jackson were, officially, never heard of again.

'Judas' Jim Murphy died in agony from drinking poison a year after betraying Sam Bass. Whether it was suicide, accidental, or murder was never gone into. Most people suspected the latter.

As for Clint and Teresa, George and Kathleen Piper, they were, of course, fictional. But, you never know, somebody must have had the money. Unless it's still hidden under some rattlesnake infested rocks someplace?